LINDA BYLER

LITTLE AMISH LIZZIE

THE BUGGY SPOKE SERIES

book one

Good Books

New York, New York

LITTLE AMISH LIZZIE

Copyright © 2018 by Linda Byler

Good Books books may be purchased in bulk at special discounts for sales promotion, corporate gifts, fund-raising, or educational purposes. Special editions can also be created to specifications. For details, contact the Special Sales Department, Good Books, 307 West 36th Street, 11th Floor, New York, NY 10018 or info@skyhorsepublishing.com.

Good Books is an imprint of Skyhorse Publishing, Inc.®, a Delaware corporation.

Visit our website at www.goodbooks.com.

10 9 8 7 6 5 4 3 2 1

Library of Congress Cataloging-in-Publication Data is available on file.

ISBN: 978-1-68099-356-1
eBook ISBN: 978-1-68099-358-5

Cover design by Jenny Zemanek

Printed in Canada

To my husband, Gideon,
for having faith in my ability
to write when I had none.

contents

preface

I suppose it is only truthful to say that my love of the Laura Ingalls series is what prompted me to write about Lizzie. I hope lots of little girls will love Lizzie and her family as much as I loved the *Little House* books as a child.

I don't know if Lizzie would ever have come into being if Mrs. Jerre Esh would not have taken the time to write a letter of encouragement. I think it was one of those little acts of kindness that we do, never knowing what we have done. That, definitely, was the deciding factor to get me started.

Most of the incidents in Lizzie's life are true, although the story is rounded out with imaginary conversations and happenings. The fears, thoughts, and attitudes, however, are very real.

— LINDA BYLER

chapter 1

A Kitten Named Snowball

Little Lizzie Glick sat beside the white picket fence and looked and looked at the white kitten. The kitten was quite perfect, with big blue eyes, a pink tongue, and the softest, whitest fur anyone could imagine.

Lizzie's sister Emma sat holding the kitten in her lap, softly stroking its fur. Lizzie wondered if Emma really liked the kitten as much as she let on. For some reason, that little kitten just gave Lizzie the biggest knot in her stomach. She actually felt quite sick. She searched Emma's face, desperately looking for a sign that she felt the same.

Emma looked just like Emma. Small and round, with dark hair rolled up at the side and put into a little round bob in the back as was the fashion of all little Amish girls. Her green dress was covered with white cat hair and she looked absolutely content.

What is wrong with me? Lizzie wondered. *I don't even want this kitten. I just know it will come to a tragic end.* Finally, she could admit to herself what the knot in her stomach was all about. She was afraid. Desperately afraid. Things like this just happened . . . a car would drive over it, or it could drown in the creek behind their house. Or—horror of horrors—it could get into the belt of the big sewing machine in Dat's harness shop. Dat

was always busy, always in a hurry, sewing harnesses, and if that little kitten got into the shop, the end of it would be too awful to bear.

Lizzie sniffed nervously. She smoothed her dark red dress over her little round stomach and put a strand of brown hair behind her ear. She looked up at the sky and thought of anything else she could: clouds, or tree branches, or God, and wondered why little white kittens were even allowed to be.

Suddenly she could take it no longer. "Emma!" she burst out.

Emma jumped and looked up in surprise. "Lizzie, what?"

"Emma . . . oh . . . nothing." Lizzie hung her head miserably.

"What's wrong, Lizzie? Do you want to hold Snowball awhile?"

"No, no! You can have her!"

Emma looked at Lizzie quite closely. "Lizzie, don't you like Snowball? You act like you're actually afraid of her!"

"Oh, be quiet, Emma. Of course I'm not afraid of her."

"Well, you act so stupid."

Lizzie jumped up, put her hands on her hips, leaned forward, and glared into Emma's face. "Don't you tell me I'm stupid, Emma Glick. I'm going to tell Mam right now!"

Turning on her heel, she burst into loud wails of pent-up frustration. Just as she reached the porch steps, her sister Mandy stepped carefully through the front door holding a blue dish filled with warm milk. Mam had one arm extended to keep the door open so Mandy could pass through.

Mam's kind face held a look of concern and pity. She came through the door and held out her arms. "Come here, Lizzie. What's wrong with my Lizzie now?"

Lizzie buried her face in Mam's warm apron which smelled of clean wash and pie crusts. Mam was so soft

with her plump figure and round face. Just like a soft
pillow you could lay your head into and cry till you were
done—which Lizzie proceeded to do while Mam stroked
her brown hair and adjusted a stray hairpin on her
straggly little bob.

Sniffing and hiccuping, sobbing and crying, she clung
tight to Mam while Emma plopped down on the wooden
porch steps, still hugging Snowball. Mandy just stood
there, looking forlorn and skinny, with her huge green
eyes first on Lizzie, then Emma, on to Snowball, and
last, to the little dish of milk.

"I don't know what in the whole world came over her,
Mam. She just acts so dumb about Snowball. She won't
even hold her. She's always so weird." Emma sniffed
and lowered her lashes as if to remind Mam how pathet-
ic Lizzie actually was.

Lizzie pulled back from Mam's apron, which had
a big wet splotch on it from all Lizzie's tears. Anger
put a quick stop to her flow of sorrow, and she turned
and slapped Emma hard, directly on her cheek. Emma
snapped back in surprise, and Snowball jumped out of
her lap immediately.

"You don't know what's wrong with me. You don't
even know if anything *is* wrong. So just be quiet!"

"Lizzie!" Mam reached down to get a firm grip on her
shoulder. "You apologize to Emma right now. If you
don't, I'm going to get Dat."

Mandy had set down the bowl of milk and ran to
scoop up Snowball. She held the kitten tightly, and
rolled her big green eyes at Lizzie.

Lizzie stood defiantly. Her whole being churned with feelings of indecision. Should she apologize nicely, cry again, and tell Mam all of her fears? But they were so stupid. Lizzie really hated herself. Why did her imagination have to make life so miserable? Why couldn't she just love Snowball and cuddle her with Emma and laugh and be happy? Why did she even have to think horrible thoughts of a car squashing Snowball, or her wet little head struggling in the fast-flowing waters of the creek? Wasn't she normal at all?

Mam's grip on her shoulders tightened. "Say you're sorry, Lizzie."

Lizzie faced Emma. Oh, that Emma. There she stood in all her . . . her goodness. She looked so . . . so untroubled and calm. And if she had any idea what was in Lizzie's head she would laugh and call her a chicken. Which, Lizzie guessed, is really exactly what she was. A chicken. Well, a chicken could stand up for herself. So Lizzie stood tall, looked Emma straight in the eye, and said, "Sorry." With that, she bent, picked up Snowball, and stalked off as fast as her chubby legs could go.

She must have held the kitten too tightly because Snowball meowed, spit, and scratched Lizzie horribly. Lizzie threw down the kitten, which ran off into Mandy's welcoming arms and back to her warm bowl of milk.

"Lizzie, what did you do to her?" Emma yelled.

"Nothing!"

"Yes, you did!"

"Did not!"

"Girls, if you don't straighten up about this little kitten, it is going right back to Doddys' farm. And I mean it. Emma and Lizzie—both of you—it's time to come set the table for supper." Mam turned and went into the house.

Lizzie picked a hairpin out of her bob and jerked her head, hard. She scuffed a toe into the gravel of the driveway and wished she could just die. But maybe that wouldn't be good just then, as much as she hated Emma.

.   .   .   .   .

The large round moon rose slowly in the dark night sky. Little white stars twinkled in the summer night, and a breeze ruffled the clean white curtain in the upstairs bedroom window of the small two-story shingled house where Lizzie lived.

The creek wound like a silver ribbon behind the house, softly babbling to itself as it splashed over rocks and made little ripples in the low places. The road that went past Lizzie's house made a turn and went over the bridge, past Doddy Glicks' farm. Doddy and Mommy Glick had a large family and a busy farm, which in the night scene looked serene and peaceful. This was Lizzie's world, and at five years old, it was a big world, full of adventures every day.

Now as a moonbeam spread across her bed, she blinked her eyes and wondered if the moon would be just as bright tomorrow night. She thought the moon just made the night more scary, especially if you couldn't sleep to begin with.

She sincerely hoped Snowball the kitten was sound asleep, and not out in the yard running around in the moonlight. She could go out on the road, and some late passerby could hit her with his car.

Lizzie sighed and flipped on her side, punching her pillow with a little round fist. She wished she could sleep. Emma lay beside her sound asleep, her breathing an even rhythm. Lizzie wished she was Emma. Emma didn't worry about things like Lizzie did. She didn't even think about scary things and awful things that could happen.

And Mam just didn't understand all Lizzie's worries, because Lizzie was too ashamed to tell her. So she tossed and turned some more, thinking about white kittens and what could happen to them.

Finally she could not take one more minute of this thinking. She sat straight up, took one look at Emma's sleeping form, and hopped out of bed. The moon made a path of light as she stuck her tousled head around the bedroom door, peering down the hallway.

Could she do this? Yes, she could, and off she tiptoed as quietly as possible—down the stairs, one at a time, and into the kitchen. She reached the laundry room door, and slowly opened it, her heart pounding in her throat. Reaching down, she slowly felt for Snowball in the cardboard box beside the washing machine.

Just as her fingers touched Snowball's soft coat, a blinding light shone in behind her.

"Ooh!" Lizzie yelped and jumped up.

Mam stood there, holding a big green flashlight as her other hand clutched at her housecoat.

"Lizzie! What are you doing out of your bed at this time of the night?"

Lizzie looked down ashamedly. "I just couldn't sleep, Mam. I was worried about Snowball and wondered if she was alright. Does . . . does that matter?"

Mam knelt down and gathered Lizzie into her arms. She smelled so good and felt so wonderful that instantly tears came to Lizzie's eyes.

"Lizzie, Lizzie, my funny, worried little girl. Were you lying up there worrying yourself about this kitten? Don't you know that God takes care of all His creatures? Even sparrows and worms and especially kittens."

"But . . . but . . . they *do* die sometimes, don't they?"

Mam stroked Lizzie's hair and held her close while she told her all about how God knows and cares about everything and that little girls could sleep peacefully every night because God loved Snowball, too.

Lizzie sniffed and relaxed against Mam. And as Mam held her hand and went back upstairs with her, tucking her in beside Emma, Lizzie could hardly bear the feeling of love she felt for Mam.

Wasn't it just wonderful that even if God allowed kittens to be, He also made soft, warm Mams who smelled like talcum powder and whose soft housecoat felt like she imagined Heaven would feel?

She only blinked at the moonlight once before she fell into a deep, lovely sleep.

The Harness Shop

Lizzie poked her fork into the soft, runny center of her "dippy" egg. She had half of her buttered toast in her other hand and as soon as the soft, warm yolk ran out, she quickly dipped a corner of her toast to catch it.

The morning sun shone warmly into the cozy little white kitchen. The blue and white tiles on the floor shone with the fresh coat of wax Mam had given it on Friday. The table stood against one wall, with a bench behind it, where Lizzie, Emma, and Mandy were seated. Mam sat at one end of the table and Dat at the other, with a glass pitcher of orange juice catching the sun's rays.

Dat handed the jelly to Emma, and she proceeded to spread it on her toast. Emma always made sure every little area of toast was evenly spread with jelly, and she was still spreading it while Lizzie took big mouthfuls of egg and toast.

Dat's brown hair and beard were neatly combed and he had on a freshly laundered green shirt. Because he worked in his harness shop, his skin was always pale, and his gray-blue eyes crinkled as he watched Emma carefully spread her jelly.

"Emma, isn't your egg going to be cold till you have that jelly spread evenly?" he asked with a smile.

Emma looked up, the concentration still in her eyes. "Oh, no. I'm done now, Dat."

"Why does it take you so long?" Dat asked.

Emma frowned. "'Cause I hate to bite into a piece of toast with too much crust and not enough jelly." She sat up straighter, picked up her fork, and carefully cut a piece of egg, adjusting it exactly on one square of her toast.

"Yuck!" Without thinking, Lizzie voiced her opinion of the jelly mixed with the egg. "How can you eat that?"

"I'll say," Mandy piped up.

Emma looked down her nose at her two younger sisters while she chewed slowly and serenely, enjoying her breakfast. She didn't bother giving them a reply, and that really irked Lizzie. She hadn't fallen asleep as early as usual because of Snowball, and here was Emma, acting like a queen again. She took a sip of orange juice and looked away, determined not to talk if Emma didn't.

"Well, I think if you are so proper about your jelly, maybe you could learn to help me make harnesses today," Dat said. "You know how I put flaxseed in the crupper, the part that goes under the horse's tail to hold the harness across its back? I'll bet you could do that just perfectly."

"Oh, goody! Yes, of course, Dat, I want to!" Emma was all excited.

"Good. After you help Mam with the dishes, you can come out to the shop. Now let's put patties down, so we can go."

"Putting patties down" was an Amish ritual at every meal. Children were taught at a young age to fold their hands under the table, and bow their heads while they thought a silent prayer of thanksgiving for their food. They did this before and after every meal.

Lizzie was not very devout. She would often forget to pray, and think other things while everyone else bowed their heads lower than she did. It wasn't that she wanted to be that way. She just figured it was okay—God knew she thought her egg and toast were good.

After the silent prayer, Dat got up, pushed back his chair, and told the girls he'd see them in a little while.

Mam sat drinking her coffee, and watched them while they hurried through clearing the table.

Lizzie yelled, "Wash! Wash! My turn to wash!"

Emma was carrying the glasses to the sink. She turned around and said, "Not so loud, Lizzie. So what? I don't want to wash. Go ahead and wash!"

"Good. I wasn't going to let you," Lizzie told her.

"So. I am going to learn how to make harnesses today, and you're too little, anyway," Emma replied.

Lizzie squeezed the bottle of dish detergent so hard that she had entirely too many suds in the sink.

Mam looked over her shoulder. "Lizzie, not so much soap. You'll never get those dishes rinsed properly."

"But, Mam, if you look at pictures, the soapsuds are way over the sink. English people use much more soap than Amish people do."

Mam hid her smile while she assured Lizzie that was probably an advertisement, and because Lizzie did not know what that was, Mam had to explain every detail of an advertisement.

Dishes done, the girls skipped out the sidewalk and across the gravel drive to the harness shop. As they burst through the door, Lizzie inhaled deeply. She just loved the sights and smells of the harness shop. Along one wall were shelves lined with all kinds of boxes of shoes. The corner next to the shoes had a steel pole with arms, called a saddle tree. It looked like a huge tree and every branch held a saddle. There were black saddles and brown ones, tan ones, and fancy ones. The fancy saddles were all carved with designs and had lots of silver and tassels dangling from them. You could push one saddle and the whole tree revolved so you could look closely at the one you wanted.

There were halters, bridles, neck ropes, liniments, and shampoos. Everything Dad had in his shop was about horses and ponies—except for the shoes; they were for people's feet, and Lizzie never tired of watching customers try on new shoes.

There was a counter with a cash register and different little racks of snacks. Candy, crackers, and potato chips were all piled neatly in sections. Across from the snacks was a big red cooler with the words *"Coca-Cola"* written in big white letters slanted at an angle. Lizzie could never quite figure that out. Why would you write that so crooked? If you really wanted to know what it said, you had to hold your head crooked, too. The big red cooler was filled with chunks of ice and deep black water that was so cold it hurt your hand if you touched it. Bottles of Coca-Cola, 7-Up, and orange and grape soda floated around in the ice-cold water. But Emma and Lizzie were very seldom allowed to have soda. It was always a special treat when Dat smiled, his eyes twinkled, and he fished in the cold water for their favorite orange flavor.

Today Dat was very busy. He sat behind the counter of his big green sewing machine that sewed the shiny black harnesses. The motor out behind the shop made a steady sound—flub, flub, flub—providing the power to run the big heavy needle up and down. The floor was strewn with bits and pieces of leather and string. Usually the shop was swept clean, but if Dat was really busy, as he was today, it looked a mess.

Emma and Lizzie stepped close and touched his arm. His face broke into a happy grin. He stopped the machine, swiveled on his stool, and said, "There are my girls! All done with the dishes already?"

Lizzie hopped up and down. "Can I help, too, Dat?"

Dat got out his shiny black and brown pipe. He scooped up a pipeful of tobacco and tamped it down with his thumb. He put the pipe in his mouth, struck a match on the seat of his stool, and put it to the tobacco. As he inhaled through the pipe, the tobacco became a red fuzzy glow. Lizzie loved to watch Dat do this, and loved the smell of the pipe smoke.

After he had blown out the smoke, he looked at
Lizzie, but he was not smiling. She just knew what he
was going to say, and her heart sank.

"Lizzie, dear, I'm just afraid you're too small. When
you're as old as Emma, I'll let you help, okay? You can
get the broom and sweep the shop if you want to help
me."

Lizzie looked at the floor and kicked a piece of leather. She clenched her hands hard behind her back so
she wouldn't cry. The lump in her throat felt as big and
scratchy as a walnut, but she blinked, swallowed hard,
and whispered, "Okay."

Dat squeezed her shoulder with his hand and said,
"That's my girl, Lizzie. You just have to grow a bit taller
and be a bit older."

"Yeah, Lizzie, I'll be in first grade next year, you
know. I am the oldest, so why don't you go get the
broom and start sweeping?"

Lizzie's head flew up as a hot anger gripped her whole
being. "Just *shut up*, Emma! You think you are *always*
better and bigger than I am. I can run faster than you,
anyway!" Lizzie clenched her fists as she hurled the biggest insult.

Dat's hand came down firmly on Lizzie's shoulder,
and Lizzie knew she had gone too far.

The little bell above the door tinkled merrily as the
first customer of the day entered the shop. It was a big
Mennonite man whom Dat was well acquainted with.

Forgetting the girls' unhappiness, Dat's hand fell
away from Lizzie's shoulder, and he straightened up,

putting his pipe back in his mouth. After exhaling, his face broke into a big smile. "Well, Paul, what brings you here this morning? I haven't seen you in a long time!"

The big Mennonite man looked closely at Dat's pipe and stated loudly, "Melvin, when are you going to give up that bad habit?"

Dat took the pipe out of his mouth and looked at it sheepishly. "Oh, I don't know, Paul. I . . ."

"Well, you know they're finding out more and more that smoking causes cancer of the lungs. And lung cancer is a big killer in the United States. Every time you suck on that stem you're making your lungs as black as coal. And if you ever could see the lungs of a cadaver that smoked, you would throw that pipe as far as you could and never touch it again.

"Besides, it's wrong in the sight of God, too, which is a lot worse!"

Dat grinned self-consciously.

"Yes, Paul, of course I think you're right. But once you've been smoking tobacco as long as I have, you would understand how hard it is to quit."

"It's the devil, Melvin. You're just not being careful enough of the devil," Paul boomed.

Lizzie felt her face turn white. She felt dizzy and sick to her stomach. She threw a terrified glance at Emma, who was calmly watching the exchange between the two men while she picked up pieces of leather. Didn't Emma hear what that Mennonite man said? This was the most terrible thing Lizzie had ever heard.

Without thinking, she turned, twisted the doorknob blindly, and slipped through the door. She ran desperately, on shaking legs, across the gravel drive and up the sidewalk, and hurled her little body on the glider which stood on the porch.

Her mind raced and her heart beat so rapidly, she wondered if fear ever made someone die.

How could her beloved Dat's lungs be completely black? She pictured her Dat, cold and quite dead, and a doctor opening his chest and and finding his lungs as black as coal. She shivered. She drew up her knees, pulled down her skirt, and buried her face in her dress.

Terror pounded in her chest and threatened to choke her. And then yet . . . oh, how unthinkable—that man said that the devil had got her Dat. Well, not really got him, but the same as that. What did he mean by saying it wasn't right in the sight of God? Did he mean God did not like it when Dat lit his pipe? Or was the devil so close to Dat that God couldn't see him clearly?

Oh, this was awful. Why was she even in the shop? Why did that Paul have to say those things? She was much too scared to cry. Her mouth was as dry as sandpaper, and her breath came in short, hot gasps. Maybe if she wouldn't have called Emma names, Paul would have driven past the harness shop and never came in the door. She was pretty sure it wasn't God who made her tell Emma to shut up, so that left only the devil. She was so scared of the devil, she could never think of him. She had already found that if you started to think of him, and you thought of cupcakes or pancakes or anything good, it would go away. So she sat on the glider and thought of pancakes. A big stack of at least four fluffy golden brown pancakes, with a dot of butter and piles of syrup running down the sides.

The harness shop, Paul the Mennonite man, Dat and his pipe, and Emma learning to put flaxseed into cruppers while Lizzie had to sweep, all faded away and seemed quite unimportant.

But probably there were guardian angels at work, so one very sensitive little Lizzie could remain a child who was only five years old.

And she never told a single soul.

Playing House

Emma and Lizzie sat at their little play table, holding their dolls. Emma's doll was named Mary, but Lizzie thought that was a very plain name for a doll, so she named her doll Reneé because it sounded so English.

Lizzie thought it made her doll seem a bit classy to be called Reneé. She didn't really want to be English herself, but she loved to watch English people talk and listen to their slang, admiring their clothes and flashes of jewelry.

Mam loved all her English neighbors, and they often took her grocery shopping, or just sat in the kitchen drinking coffee.

This afternoon Lizzie plopped Reneé on her lap and said, "Reneé, why are you spilling all your food?"

Emma looked up from feeding Mary with a little play

spoon. She giggled and told Lizzie if Reneé was a real baby she couldn't plop her down so hard.

Lizzie giggled back. They crunched their soda crackers and soaked them with milk, feeding their babies and talking their little mother language.

It was a drizzly, wet day outside. But inside their little playhouse everything was cozy. The playhouse itself was actually an old building close to the house. It was not really a shed, because it had tiny little creaky stairs that went up to a second story.

Lizzie would have loved to have a little bedroom upstairs and actually use the creaky old stairs, but Dat closed the opening at the top because too many bumblebees had nests up there. If Lizzie climbed up the stairs she could hear the low buzzing, and she was dreadfully afraid of all those bumblebees.

Downstairs the floor was made of wide wooden planks with knotholes in them. Sometimes when Lizzie swept the floor, she would try and sweep all the dirt down through one knothole. Emma would fuss and scold, but Lizzie thought it was fun, going 'round and 'round the knothole with her broom.

The girls had a play table with three little wooden chairs, a little wooden cupboard filled with dishes, some brightly colored rugs Mam had given them, and a little bed for their dolls. They still needed curtains for their windows, but Mam just didn't have time to make them.

Lizzie loved the playhouse. Today the rain made a soft, pattery sound on the metal roof, and Emma was so nice to her; she even gave Lizzie one of Mary's toys to keep.

They decided together that Lizzie would be English and would come to visit Emma, who would be Amish.

"I could actually dress up in English clothes," Lizzie said.

"We don't have any, Lizzie. Besides, Mam would never let you. That would be stupid," Emma said.

Lizzie thought awhile. She could wear her nightie and put her hair in a ponytail. But Emma would think that was stupid, too, so she didn't say anything.

She looked down at her plain brown dress and her bare feet peeping out underneath. She could at least wear shoes if she was going to be English.

"I know what, Emma! I can use my doll's beads for a necklace. I'm going to." Lizzie ran to her doll purse and found a string of beads. She let it slide over her head and patted them on her chest. They looked bright yellow and glittered against her plain brown dress, and suddenly

Lizzie felt so English. Now she needed shoes — wouldn't it feel really neat to have high heels?

"Emma, you know what?" Lizzie sighed.

"What?"

"Why won't Mam buy us those glittery pink and purple play shoes in a package? It would be alright to wear them if we stayed in the playhouse and no one would see us, wouldn't it?" asked Lizzie.

Emma, who was always the practical one, put her hands on her hips and faced Lizzie squarely, saying, "Yes, but Lizzie, you know she would if we weren't Amish. We aren't allowed to have fancy shoes and suppose she would buy them and later we just kept wearing shoes like that when we're big? Then we wouldn't even really be Amish right, and that would break Mam and Dat's heart."

Lizzie flicked back a stray strand of hair and told Emma, "They could get used to it."

Emma scolded, "Now Lizzie, just forget about those shoes. You know you're not allowed to have them, so just forget it. You're so . . . oh, whatever. C'mon, let's play."

Lizzie sat up. "Okay. I'll be the English lady, but I have to get shoes. I'll be back," she said as she dashed out the door and raced through the raindrops to the kitchen door. It slammed behind her as she stood scraping her bare feet on the rug.

She heard Mam laugh and talk in English. Lizzie peeped around the cupboard and saw Mrs. Bixler, the lady who owned the little grocery store, sitting at the kitchen table with some homemade cinnamon rolls on a plate beside her.

She was a tall, good-looking woman in her early forties. Her hair was cut short and shone under the gas light, and her earrings sparkled every time she turned her head. She had on a dark green skirt with a crisp white blouse and her shoes were the greatest wonder of all. They were white and had high heels. Oh, how Lizzie would have loved to try walking in those wonderful shoes!

Mam caught sight of Lizzie at the same moment Mrs. Bixler did.

"Why, Lizzie, there you are!" Mrs. Bixler boomed. "How's my little girl? You come here and give me a nice hug."

Lizzie just stood on the rug and gazed at her shyly.

Mrs. Bixler opened her arms and Lizzie walked slowly to her. She was soon enveloped in a big warm hug, and the ruffles on her white blouse tickled Lizzie's nose. She felt embarrassed, but Mrs. Bixler smelled so wonderful, and Lizzie wondered if it was perfume or talcum powder like Mam used.

Mrs. Bixler held Lizzie at arm's length and exclaimed, "My gosh, Lizzie, you are really growing. And where did you find those pretty yellow beads?"

Lizzie's face turned pink and her cheeks felt hot, but she bravely shrugged her shoulders and said in perfect English, "In my doll purse."

Mam beamed to hear Lizzie speak in good English. Amish children learned to speak Pennsylvania Dutch first, but by age six or seven, most of them could speak reasonably well in English. They usually mastered both languages at a young age, although Dutch was naturally easier.

Mam smiled at Lizzie and asked, "Are you still playing in the playhouse?"

Lizzie clasped her hands behind her back, smiled, and said, "Yes."

Mrs. Bixler clapped her hands. "Good job, Lizzie! You can speak English well!"

She turned to Mam and said, "My stars! Before you know it Lizzie will be a grown young lady. Speaking English already! Goodness!"

Mam smiled at Mrs. Bixler and replied. "Yes, I know. Emma is going to school this fall—or she should go, although I'm not sure if we will send her. She won't be six till November, and we're just not sure yet."

Lizzie was safely out of Mrs. Bixler's grasp now, so she backed quietly away and walked slowly toward the laundry room, where her shoes were kept.

She heard Mam say, "Lizzie, I'll bring Mandy out to you when she wakes from her nap."

"Okay, we're in the playhouse," Lizzie answered as she splashed back through the rain to Emma.

Emma looked up when Lizzie entered. "Where were you so long, Lizzie? We have to start playing 'cause you know how it goes when Mandy wakes up. Then we have to play with her, too, and she never wants to be my child."

"She's still sleeping. Mam will bring her out when she

wakes up. Hey, you know who was there? Mrs. Bixler.
She's so pretty and looks so nice and smells so good,
and she gave me a hug. And, Emma, you should just see
her shoes. They're white and have high heels and are all
shiny white."

Emma just snorted.

Lizzie said, "Well, you just don't know how pretty
those shoes were. And you know what, Emma? She
says, 'Oh, my stars!' That sounds so . . . I don't know—
so much like an English lady. When I come visit you I
can say that, 'cause I'll be English."

Lizzie stood straight and tall and said, "My stars!" as
clearly as she could.

Emma looked at Lizzie and frowned. "Lizzie, I mean
it. You are so different. You know you are not allowed
to say that. It sounds so . . . I don't know. First you want
English shoes and now you say that. I'm going to tell
Mam if you don't stop acting so English."

Lizzie said, "Emma, I am not English for real. I don't
even know what you mean."

"Oh, well, forget it. You go outside now and knock,
then I'll open the door, okay?"

Lizzie was sitting on the floor, looking at the soles
of her shoes. She was concentrating so hard, she didn't
hear Emma.

"Lizzie!" Emma exclaimed loudly.

"What?"

"C'mon. What are you doing?"

Lizzie jumped up. "I know just what. I need two
blocks of wood to tie onto my shoes and I'll have high

heels. I'm going to the woodshed to see if I can find some to make me some high-heeled shoes." With that she dashed out into the rain.

Emma sat down dejectedly. Why did Lizzie have to be so different? A lot of things she thought of just didn't make sense to Emma. What did she get out of saying that, and why in the world did she have to be so desperate to wear high heels that she would go get blocks of wood?

So Emma waited, and finally got a coloring book and crayons from the cupboard. She found a really nice picture of a squirrel in a tree and selected a green crayon. She became so engrossed in her coloring, she forgot all about Lizzie, so the knock on the door came as a bit of a surprise. *Oh yes, that's Lizzie,* she thought as she got up to open the door.

"Hello!" Lizzie boomed very loudly. "How are you, Emma?"

Lizzie was way too tall. Emma's gaze traveled from Lizzie's beaming face to her shoes. Sure enough, she had a block of wood tied securely with baler twine over the top of her foot.

Emma immediately played along, extending her hand and saying, "Why, come just in, Mrs. Bixler! I'm just fine. And where did you get your new high-heeled shoes?"

Lizzie held her head up high, and in a genuine English lady imitation, she said, "Oh, I just bought them at the store!"

They both collapsed on the floor in a fit of giggles. When Lizzie hit the floor, her high heels fell apart, which had them laughing much more.

Emma sputtered, "L-L-Lizzie—your shoes!"

Lizzie gasped, "Well, they did feel like high heels a little bit. Now if you would just let me say, 'Oh, my stars!'"

Emma's laughter disappeared and she looked squarely at Lizzie, her smile completely gone.

"You just have to say that, Lizzie. Go ask Mam if you may. Go on. See what she says. Or go sit in a corner and keep saying it—see how good it feels."

Lizzie pondered this for a while. She picked up the blocks of wood and twine, trying to reattach them to her shoes.

She looked at Emma. "There's hardly any use, is there? These aren't really high heels, and I'm not really English. But we had fun, didn't we, Emma?"

Emma smiled and put her hand in Lizzie's. "C'mon, you silly little girl. Let's go see if Mam has any cinnamon rolls left. Maybe Mandy's awake, too."

Lizzie squeezed Emma's hand and loved her so much she thought her heart would burst. Dear, bossy big sister Emma.

chapter 4

Marvin and Elsie

Emma and Lizzie were on their way to Grandpa Glicks' farm. They walked carefully on the gravel path beside the road, pulling their little red express wagon.

The late afternoon sun slanted through the trees, and birds twittered and trilled their various songs as they made their way up the small grade that led across the bridge. The waters of the creek sounded like a "fussy little song," as Emma put it.

The girls stopped, balancing on their tiptoes to peep across the thick stone wall. Lizzie always had a feeling of delicious fear, thinking of jumping off that stone wall. How would it feel if she just jumped right off and landed with her feet in the rippling water below? But the only trouble was, she couldn't be sure of landing on her feet. Suppose she would slowly do a flip and land on her head? At any rate, her stomach felt too full of butterflies to even think about it, so she just stared at the water and was so glad she was safely behind the wall.

There was a tin gallon jug with a swinging handle on the wagon, packed into a cardboard box. Grandpa Glicks had a dairy farm with a herd of black and white Holsteins providing milk. So whenever Mam's container of milk was almost gone, Emma and Lizzie were allowed to walk to Grandpas to fill the tin jug. They never had to take money, because Grandma wrote it on the tablet which hung beside her refrigerator in the kitchen, and Dat would "settle up" every month.

Lizzie was so happy because they were allowed to stay for an hour and play with Marvin and Elsie. Marvin was a few years older, but Elsie was about the same age as Emma.

Elsie was actually Emma's aunt, which seemed different, but Grandpa Glicks had a large family of fourteen children. Dat had explained to Emma that since he was the oldest, he married Mam, and they had Baby Emma,

and Grandma's last baby was Elsie. So it was a really
neat thing, Lizzie always thought, because she loved to
go to Grandpa Glicks' house to play with Marvin and
Elsie.

Emma hopped off the ledge that ran along the stone
wall of the bridge.

"Ready, Lizzie?"

"Yep!" Lizzie jumped down. Each of the girls put one
hand in the curved handle of the wagon and were on
their way. Down the small hill, around the bend, and
they came to the mailbox that said "Samuel Glick".

Pink and purple flowers were planted neatly in a little
area surrounded by stone. The mailbox was painted
bright silver and was supported on a thick white post.
Everything on Grandpa Glicks' farm was kept very
neat. The buildings were painted a fresh coat of white
paint, the lawn trimmed to precision, and the gravel
drive was properly raked every Saturday, so no straw or
hay was strewn across it.

Emma and Lizzie were always a little in awe of
Grandma Glick. She was a friendly grandma, who always smiled at them and was glad to see them, but usually didn't stay still very long. She was always working,
her hands busy baking bread, shelling peas, washing
dishes, or some other important
task.

So when Emma and Lizzie reached the yard, they plopped down the handle of the wagon and ran up the sidewalk, eager to see Grandma Glick.

The wide porch floor was painted dark gray, and there was a neat black rubber mat that said "Welcome" in front of the door.

They could smell some wondrous smell coming from the oven just inside the door.

Emma opened the door a little and said, "Grandma! Are you home?"

Lizzie hopped up and down on the rubber mat because it tickled her bare feet.

Grandma came rushing to the door, wiping her hands on her gray apron. Her hair was still dark brown with very little gray in it, and her brown eyes crinkled as she smiled at the girls.

"Come in, Emma—you don't have to knock! Come in, Lizzie! How are my girls this afternoon?"

"What are you baking, Grandma?" Lizzie asked.

Grandma's hearty laugh rang out. "Ach, Lizzie, you are more concerned about what's in my oven than saying hello to me! You're getting just as plump as a little partridge, too." She reached down and patted Lizzie's soft stomach. "Does Mam make you good things to eat?"

Lizzie smiled up at Grandma, self-consciously shrugging her shoulders. Her thick, dark lashes swept her cheeks and she blushed a little girl pink color.

"Yes, Grandma, she does."

The door opened and Marvin and Elsie burst through, their clothes covered with hay dust and their faces

streaked with sweat and dirt.

Marvin had reddish-blond curly hair, with an old torn straw hat smashed down until his ears turned down slightly at the top. His nose was funny looking. Instead of being straight along the top like other people's, it had a bump that made his nose look like he had run into a brick wall. But crooked nose or not, Lizzie loved Uncle Marvin, and would go to great lengths to impress him.

Elsie was small, with curly hair, too. But her hair was rolled back tightly, like all little Amish girls, so it had little plastered-down waves. She had gray eyes and was dressed in a navy blue dress made from one of her older sisters' dresses.

She smiled at Emma and Lizzie, looping her arm through Emma's. "Hi! Guess what Marvin and I are doing?"

Lizzie hopped up and down. "What? What?"

Elsie stood up straight and took a deep breath. "Why, we're—"

"Jumping in the haymow!" Marvin's loud voice interrupted Elsie.

"Marvin! I was going to say it. Lizzie, we're just about—"

"Hey," Marvin cut in again. "Hey! We stacked all the bales around to form a huge tunnel. And at the—"

"There's a huge room," Elsie chimed in, "with even a window and a hole in the roof, to let the air in."

"Or out," Marvin said.

"G-oo-oody!" Lizzie clapped her hands and squealed. "That sounds like so much fun! Let's go!"

Emma, always the practical one, remembered the time Dat had told them to come home.

"But, Lizzie, we really can't stay too long. Dat said we may stay for one hour, and then we have to take the milk home. Mam needs it for supper."

Marvin and Lizzie were already out the door and running across the porch. Elsie was in hot pursuit, and Emma glanced hurriedly at the kitchen clock, but she really couldn't tell time anyway. A hurried thought of telling Grandma what time they were supposed to be home entered her mind, but she saw Elsie dashing after Marvin and Lizzie, and Emma was soon flying down the porch steps after them.

Four little figures went racing down the gravel drive, past the buggy shed and the kerosene tank, and into the milkhouse. The milkhouse was cool and damp, painted a clean white on the top, with the bottom painted a pale

blue color. Stainless steel milking machines hung on
a metal rack and a deep trough made of concrete held
dozens of steel cans of milk. You couldn't open those
cans unless you used a special hammer and tapped
under the lid. If you tapped on one side too much, the
other side wouldn't budge. But if you tapped lightly all
around the lid, it would pop off. Lizzie often wondered
why this was so. And why the cold water in the trough
stayed so cold. She was too little to know that the diesel
engine that went "putt-putt-putt" on a hot summer day
provided the power for the refrigeration.

So Lizzie always thought the water came up out of the
ground in the milkhouse.

Marvin put their little metal jug carefully beside the
rack of milkers. "Now, when it's time for you to go
home, there is your jug," he said.

Emma looked worried. "But, Marvin, how are we going to know when an hour is up? Dat said we're allowed
to stay for only an hour, because Mam needs the milk."

Marvin rubbed his nose thoughtfully. "But then we
have to go look at the clock too often. And when we're
in the hay house, it's a long way out through the tunnel."

"We can just play awhile, and after it seems too long,
we'll go look," Lizzie said.

"Okay!" Elsie smiled happily. "Let's go!"

That seemed to settle the matter of time quite effi-
ciently and they all ran up the gravel drive that went to
the barn hill. The called it the "barn hill", but it was actually only a slight grade up to the big barn doors where
the hay was kept. It was in the back of the barn, so the

front was open where the cow stable was. It was always hard for Lizzie to understand the barn. The cows had to be lower because they threw the hay down the "hay hole." But there was only a little hill up to the haymow, and it didn't seem like the haymow was on top of the cows, but it was.

The door to the haymow had a round wooden peg that you slid back to open it. Then you had to step over a heavy board because the small door was actually part of a huge swinging door, one that even Marvin was not allowed to open. Grandpa had said so, and Marvin and Elsie listened when Grandpa spoke sternly.

Today the sun shone through the cracks in the wooden siding, creating beams of light that held millions of little dust particles. The prickly hay bales were piled high, but Lizzie was surprised that the haymow was so empty.

"Marvin, where is all your hay?" she inquired.

"It's time to make hay again this week," Marvin informed her. "It's about all gone because the cows and horses ate it over the winter."

"Oh yes, I suppose so." Lizzie said.

Elsie and Emma were already at the entrance to the tunnel. "Wow! This is really a long tunnel," exclaimed Emma.

Elsie beamed. "It sure is. Who wants to go first?"

Lizzie yelled, "Me! Me!"

"No, you can't, Lizzie. I have to go first, 'cause I know the way. Sometimes you have to crawl up and sometimes it drops down, and you won't know where you're going, 'cause you were never in the tunnel," Marvin told her.

So Marvin ducked and lowered himself to all fours. "C'mon. C'mon in after me, but be careful!"

One by one the girls followed Marvin. The hay scratched their knees and hands, and the pungent odor of it stung their nostrils. But it was so exciting, going around corners and sometimes up steps made of bales.

Just when Lizzie was giggling with delight, Marvin suddenly disappeared. Elsie followed and yelled up, "Here is a hole. Do you want us to catch you?"

Lizzie shivered with fear. This was getting a bit scary, really. But when Emma tumbled down and Marvin and Elsie giggled, Lizzie supposed it couldn't be too bad. So she just pushed forward and fell into a little hole, land-

ing on top of Elsie, who yelled, "Ouch, Lizzie—get off of me!"

Lizzie tried to get off, but there were arms and legs everywhere.

"Ow, Lizzie! If you wouldn't be so fat, it wouldn't be so full of people in this hole," Elsie said.

Lizzie puffed and pushed and really tried to get off, but there was absolutely no place to go.

"Ow!" This time it was Marvin. "Lizzie, get out of this hole. I can't even breathe with you in here!"

Suddenly Lizzie was angry. The hot anger coursed through her little veins and she shouted, "Stop blaming it on me, you big babies! I hate playing in the haymow and I hate your dumb tunnel! It's hot in here and it itches! And who in the world was stupid enough to make this big hole?"

Emma squeaked tiredly, "It's not a very big hole, Lizzie!"

Elsie gasped, "Somebody has to get out of here. I can't breathe anymore!"

Marvin started to laugh. "If Emma would get her elbow out of my eye, and if Lizzie would get off of my foot, I could probably get out."

Elsie giggled helplessly, followed by a loud sneeze. Emma sneezed, too, and they promptly collapsed into a helpless fit of giggling. They sneezed and coughed, spluttering and laughing until Marvin decided it wasn't funny anymore and untangled himself.

The rest of their journey through the tunnel was quite uneventful, except for an occasional sneeze.

When they came to the actual hay house, Emma and
Lizzie were thrilled. Marvin and Elsie had made furniture from hay bales, and had blankets spread on the
hay sofa, even having a thermos of water, cookies in one
container, and pretzels in another. It was quite the cutest thing Lizzie had ever seen.

So they all decided Marvin was the Dat, Emma the
Mam, and Lizzie and Elsie were the children. They lived
in an imaginary world of poor people who lived in hay
houses, and the pretzels were squirrel meat. The water
was milk from the only cow they had, and the cookies
were pieces of deer meat from a deer that Marvin would
have shot.

They were brought back to reality quite sharply when
Marvin said, "Shhh!"

They all sat motionless and listened. From far away
came the sound of someone calling them.

"Uh-oh," Emma said. "I bet it's much later than an
hour. We forgot all about the time."

"It isn't an hour yet," Lizzie snorted.

"I bet it is." Elsie's eyes were big and worried. "We'd
better go."

Marvin was already out the hay house door and running through the haymow.

After they all got out to the barn hill, they saw Dat
come striding up to the barn. He looked very, very worried and also very unhappy.

"Do you know what time it is, Emma?" He looked
directly at Emma with his piercing eyes.

"N-n-no," Emma stammered.

"Well, it's over two hours since you girls left, and Mam is so worried. Why didn't you come home when we told you to?"

"I . . . we . . . I mean, we didn't have a clock," Lizzie said, looking at the dandelions at her feet.

"That's a very poor excuse," Dat told her. "You could have kept checking with Grandma, to see what time it was. You are not showing any responsibility or obedience. Mam is just worried sick."

Emma and Lizzie stood in abject misery while Dat filled the little tin gallon jug with milk. Dat's disappointment would have been more bearable if Marvin hadn't been standing there holding back a scornful laugh.

Lizzie wished Marvin would fall down the hay hole and the heaviest cow would fall on top of him.

Whose Fault?

It was Saturday evening and the Glick family would not be having church services in the morning. Amish people have services every two weeks, which allows for more ministers to visit other districts.

Lizzie always looked forward to these in-between Sundays. They were allowed to sleep as long as they wanted, and they ate a late, extra-delicious breakfast. Mam had all forenoon to prepare it, so they had bacon or sausage, and homemade pancakes or French toast. Sometimes she made sausage gravy with homemade biscuits and jelly, which Lizzie just loved.

After Dat helped Mam with the dishes, he would read a Bible story to them. Emma loved Bible stories, but some of them really scared Lizzie. Like David killing Goliath with a pebble—suppose she accidentally hit

Mandy with a pebble on her forehead and she would fall over dead? It was too frightening to think about, so sometimes she wished Dat wouldn't read those kind of stories, because Lizzie just worried too much.

On this Saturday evening, when Mam called Lizzie and Emma into the kitchen, Lizzie just knew what she wanted. It was time to have their neck and ears scrubbed in the kitchen, before they took their Saturday night bath.

Mam had a basin of warm soapy water, and she did Emma first because she was the oldest. Emma grimaced while Mam scrubbed her ears, clucking her tongue at the dirt behind them.

"Emma, I think you girls roll around in the dirt like little piggies," she said, scrubbing at the side of Emma's neck. "You get so dirty playing outside."

Lizzie watched and said, "Mam, we could wash our own ears now. We're old enough."

Mam pushed Emma away, and patted the table. "Your turn, Lizzie."

Lizzie covered her ears and groaned. "I wish you'd let me wash my own ears."

"Not till you're a big girl, Lizzie dear," smiled Mom, and she proceeded to scrub Lizzie's ears till Lizzie thought they must surely be bruised. Lizzie did not like to have her ears scrubbed like that, but the side of her face that was held against Mam's soft stomach felt comfortable. She loved being close to Mam. It was just the way she smelled, so safe and comforting in Lizzie's world filled with all kinds of real and imagined fears.

"There," and Mam gave Lizzie a little shove, with a pat on her shoulder. "Emma, you get the bathwater started and I'll wash Mandy's ears."

"I'll do it, I'll do it!" yelled Lizzie, and she propelled herself forward to race Emma to the bathroom. Emma turned and raced after her and they both collided against the bathroom door.

"Lizzie, stop it! Mam said me, not you. Go away!" shouted Emma.

"I can if I want to!" Lizzie yelled back. "Get away from this door!"

Mam watched from the kitchen, unsure if she wanted to yell above all that noise, or if she wanted to wait and see what the outcome would be. That Lizzie could surely be feisty for as scared as she was of everything and its shadow.

It all happened so quickly, Mam wasn't even sure what exactly occurred. Somehow, Emma tumbled through the bathroom door first, and with all her chubby little might, she slammed the door on Lizzie's two fingers. The door was almost closed, except for the fingers smashed between the wood.

Lizzie had never felt such pain. It exploded through her hand and up her arm, and her initial reaction was to scream as loud as she could. Great big wails of sheer terror tore out of her throat. It hurt so badly, she didn't remember Mam coming to scoop her up and sit on the sofa with her.

"What in the world did you do, Emma? This poor girl's fingers are absolutely smashed." Mam blew on them, rocking her back and forth, while Lizzie howled, sobbed, yelled, and hiccuped.

"Shh, shhh, Lizzie, poor baby," crooned Mam, her face filled with consternation, as she examined the chubby little fingers. The fingernails were slowly turning purple and blue as the blood rushed into the pinched areas.

Emma sat down on the other side of the couch and cast sidelong glances at Lizzie. She thought there was no way on earth those fingers were pinched that badly. Lizzie just loved to scream so she got lots of pity and attention, which she sure was getting at the moment, with Mam looking so worried and calling her "baby." Lizzie was a baby. Mam had told her to turn on the bathwater, not Lizzie, and it served Lizzie right.

And still Lizzie kept sobbing. Mam got ice cubes and put them in a bag, holding them against Lizzie's fingers, but her yelling only increased, so Mam put them away.

"Emma, go get Dat. These fingers might be broken, as swollen as they are." She frowned. "I don't know why you girls have to act this way. You have to be careful, Emma."

"Well, Mam, you told me, me-e-e—" and Emma's voice dissolved into a flood of tears. She sat way over on her side of the couch in a miserable little huddle and let her own tears flow. At least Lizzie was being held and pitied, while she was all alone on her end of the couch, with Mam glaring at her.

Now Mandy started to cry, because everybody else was crying. Mam got up, put Lizzie on the couch, and went to find Dat.

Lizzie sank back against the cushions and quit crying long enough to look at her fingers. They were huge. They thumped with every beat of her heart, and Lizzie had a horrifying thought. Her fingers were going to fall off—that's all there was to it, which started a fresh round of sobs.

Dat entered the kitchen, finding his three daughters in a lamentable state. He walked over to Lizzie first and picked her up, setting her on his knee. Mandy rushed to the safety of her mother's arms, and Emma just sat huddled in the corner of the sofa, trying to quit crying.

"What happened, Emma?"

Emma took a deep breath, and smoothed back her hair with both hands. "Mam told me to get the bathwater ready, and Lizzie tried to do it first, and Mam told me to do it. So I got in first and pushed the bathroom door shut so she couldn't get in. It's not my fault her fingers were there!"

Dat looked sternly at both of them. He ran his fingers through his hair and frowned. After that he picked up Lizzie's fingers and frowned some more.

"No, Lizzie, I don't think your fingers are broken. They're just smashed. Your fingernails will probably come off because the force of the pinch loosened them. You'll be alright and it will help if you let Mam put ice on again."

Mam brought the ice again and held it over the injured fingers, with a soft towel wrapped around Lizzie's hand. Her sobs slowly faded as she lay back against the pillow on the sofa.

"So, Lizzie, don't you think the next time Mam tells Emma to start the water in the bathtub, you should let her do it?" Dat asked.

Lizzie's fingers hurt so horribly, and here was Dat, trying to blame her. It was Emma who pushed the door shut, and she was the one to blame.

So between hiccups and soft little "ows" and "ouches," Lizzie told Dat it was Emma's fault—not hers.

Then Dat told them a story about a greedy little pig who ate all the other little pigs' food, then got a severe stomachache and suffered for a few days, being allowed nothing but water.

Lizzie listened intently, then looked up at Dat. "You mean, I was the greedy little pig?"

"Exactly," smiled Dat. "You wanted Emma's share, and that was her job. So you got pinched fingers."

Lizzie looked long and hard at Dat. She didn't agree with him. There was no food involved in this situation. Besides, what about sharing? Emma could have let her turn on the water. In Lizzie's opinion, Emma was just as greedy as she was. Lizzie looked at Emma, and Emma looked at Lizzie, and both of them knew exactly what the other one was thinking . . . "It was your fault!"

But since Dat was there and there was no possibility of arguing, they bit their lips and glared at each other.

chapter 6

A Ride to the Mountains

The following morning the sun shone warmly through the yellow, red, and orange foliage surrounding the little shingled house where Lizzie lived.

The back door opened and she stuck her tousled little head outside, saying softly, "Here, kitty, kitty. C'mon, Snowball—time to eat!"

Snowball peeped out from under the porch and meowed. Lizzie scooped her up and set her down by the dish of milk, stroking her velvety ears as Snowball lapped at the warm, creamy milk.

Lizzie was so glad Snowball was still alive, and a car had not yet driven over her. She sat and stroked her little white kitten, yawned, and gazed at the trees by the creek. They were really bright, and she wondered how they got that way, and why they had to fall off after being so bright. She wished they could go for a long drive to see lots of pretty trees on the mountain.

She jumped up, scaring Snowball, who raced down the steps, then turned and watched Lizzie.

Lizzie ran into the house, yelling as loud as she could, "Hey! Hey, Dat!"

Mam was flipping golden brown pancakes on a smoking hot skillet. She turned and said sharply, "Shhh, Lizzie, don't be so noisy. Dat isn't here right now. He went to feed the horses."

"I'll go find him," Lizzie yelled, quite forgetting to lower her voice. Slamming the screen door, she pounded across the grass that was wet with dew. Her feet tingled with the wet coldness, and bits of grass clung to her toes as she raced across the gravel drive.

"Dat! Dat!" She was quite breathless and very noisy as she stopped inside the open barn door.

"What? What's wrong?" Dat's head appeared over the top of the wooden gate of Red's pen. He was spreading clean yellow straw around Red's feet.

"Hey! I just thought of something. You know what?" Lizzie paused and took a deep breath. "You know what, Dat?"

Dat laughed, slapping Red on the rump and pushing him over, in order to spread more straw. "Well, what?"

"You know what we should do today?" Lizzie paused, climbing up the wooden sides of Red's pen and leaning across the boards, with her elbows propped on the top.

Dat went on spreading straw, while Red's dainty ears flipped forward and back again, waiting for a command from Dat. Red was beautiful. He was a sorrel saddlebred horse, and his coat was so glossy he shone in the sunlight. When he trotted, his head was held high, while his legs lifted daintily as he moved. Lizzie thought nobody else in the whole Amish church had a horse as pretty as Red.

"Dat, how long do horses live?" she asked.

Dat smiled at her as he put his pitchfork down. "My, two questions and I don't really know the answer to any of them. Why don't you slow down and ask one thing at a time? First question—what should we do today?"

Lizzie frowned. She wasn't listening to Dat. She was watching Red eat his oats. She loved to hear a horse chew his feed. It sounded so good and crunchy, just like he was eating potato chips, and Lizzie wondered if the feed tasted as good to Red as potato chips tasted to her.

"I love chips," Lizzie commented. Dat closed the gate, hung up his fork, and came over to Lizzie. He grabbed her by her chubby little waist and lifted her down.

"You look like a little potato chip."

Lizzie laughed happily. She loved Red and she loved to watch Dat do his chores, and everything just seemed so good at that moment that she was filled with something she guessed felt like pure joy.

"I'm not a potato chip. How long do horses live?" she asked again.

"Oh, I don't know. Some of them live to be twenty-five years old, and others wear out a lot sooner. Just depends."

"Depends on what?" asked Lizzie as she watched Dat pull a piece of hay from a bale, put it in his mouth, and chew it. Lizzie did the same. If you chewed hay and bit down on the little knobby part, you could taste the sweet juice. Besides, Lizzie watched men chew hay when they worked on the farm at Grandpas. They pushed up their hat, leaned back against the fence, crossed one foot over the other and talked. Lizzie practiced it for hours, but nobody knew about it. She wished she was a man.

"Melvin! Breakfast!" Mam stood on the porch calling to them. She paused to watch them come toward the house, noticing the fact that Lizzie was chewing hay again.

That Lizzie, she thought. *I don't know why she isn't a boy, as much as she tries to act like one.*

But she didn't say anything, only smiled to herself as she watched them come up to the porch.

"Lizzie says she wants to do something today, but she hasn't said what," Dat told Mam.

Mam turned to go into the house, saying, "Well, c'mon, the pancakes and eggs will be cold if you don't hurry up."

While Lizzie sat on the bench and buttered her pancakes, she still hadn't told them her plan. She would wait, to make sure Mam wanted to go along. Sometimes Mam didn't want to go away when Lizzie did.

Emma was blowing her nose at the table. Lizzie wished she wouldn't do that. It was disgusting. Besides, Emma was grouchy this morning and made Lizzie feed Snowball first thing. So Emma really provoked Lizzie, sitting there beside her, blowing her nose as loud as she could.

Lizzie went on buttering her pancake. "Syrup," she said.

Nobody passed it.

"Syrup!" Lizzie said, more loudly.

Emma went on blowing her nose. Lizzie spied the syrup close to Emma's elbow.

"Emma, pass the syrup. And stop blowing your nose! It's gross!" Lizzie said.

Mam and Dat burst out laughing. Mam laughed till tears streamed down her face and she gasped for breath. Mandy clapped her hands and giggled, even if she didn't know what was funny.

Mam wiped her eyes, sighed, and said, "Emma, give the syrup to Lizzie."

Lizzie figured Mam and Dat were both in a very good mood, seeing them so happy, so she turned the syrup bottle upside-down and squeezed, saying, "Let's hitch up Red and go to the mountain today."

Dat smiled. "Good idea, Lizzie. The leaves are colored really pretty right now, and it's a beautiful day. Do you want to, Annie?" he asked Mam.

"We could," Mam agreed, and smiled at Dat.

"Good. After dishes and a Bible story, I'll hitch up Red and Mam can pack a lunch."

"We don't have to have a Bible story," Lizzie said.

"Oh, yes," Dat told her. "Every Sunday."

While Mam gathered the dirty dishes, putting away the leftovers, Dat sat on the couch and read the story of the lost sheep. Emma sat beside Dat and listened attentively, but Lizzie wasn't interested in that little sheep

story. So what if he didn't make it into the pen with the
others? He could stay out on the mountain till the next
morning, when the shepherd drove his sheep back that
way. Lizzie thought the shepherd wouldn't have had to
light his lantern and go look in the dark. That was a lot
scarier than waiting till morning. He was lucky he didn't
get eaten by a bear, walking around the mountain yelling for one sheep.

Now Dat was telling Emma to always remember to
be a good little girl and do as Mam said. Lizzie picked at
a scab on her knee and wished he'd be quiet now. She
wanted to go for a ride in the mountains.

After Mam packed sandwiches, apples, cookies, a jar
of peanut butter, and saltine crackers into a big picnic
basket, she combed the girls' hair while Dat put the harness on Red.

Lizzie despised having her hair combed. Mam wet
her hair, then rolled it tightly along the side of her head.
Sometimes she pulled it back so hard, Lizzie could
feel the corners of her eyes being stretched. After she
put in the ponytail holder, Lizzie propped her head on
her arms while Mam wound her long hair around and
around to make a bob, or a bun, low on the back of her
head. If you held your eyes hard against your arms long
enough, you could see stars. Then if you looked back up
and opened your eyes, you could still see them for a very
short time. Lizzie wondered why English girls could get
away without a bob.

Dat was ready, so he took a firm grip on Red's bridle
and led him to the sidewalk. Lizzie raced back and forth,

carrying the thermos jug of chocolate milk, then the blanket. She clambered up the high step and tumbled into the buggy. Emma scrambled up beside her, and they wiggled against the soft upholstered seat to make themselves comfortable. Lizzie hoped Emma wouldn't blow her nose and completely ruin her ride to the mountains.

Mam and Dat packed the lunch and all the things they needed under the seat. Mandy sat on Mam's lap while Dat clambered up beside her. He never had to tell Red to go, because the horse was always too eager. Dat could barely make it into the buggy before Red was off and running.

Gravel crunched under the steel wheels as they turned onto the main road. Emma and Lizzie could look out the back window because Dat had rolled up the gray canvas and secured the roll with leather straps that hung on a hook. They hung their elbows out the back, giggling together with excitement. *This is so fun*, Lizzie thought. She had never, ever done anything "funner."

The breeze flowed through the buggy because Dat had his window open. Mam had Mandy wrapped in a small woolen blanket, and she was laughing and telling Mam in her baby talk about the horse and buggy.

Red felt energetic and Dat had to pull back on the reins to keep him at a nice, steady pace. Red's red coat shone under the clean black harness, and the little rings jiggled to the steady "clip, clop" of his hooves.

Lizzie smelled leaves burning, and turned to look at a big pile of brown leaves. Smoke was curling up through the pile, and a man stood beside it, leaning on his rake. Dat waved and smiled as they drove past, as a little white dog ran out to the road, barking furiously.

Lizzie hated that. She was always so afraid of the horse's hooves tramping on little puppies, or the hard steel band on the wooden wheel going over the puppy's soft body. She could never stand to think about it and now she grimaced and shut her eyes tightly, just hoping as hard as she could the puppy would not be trampled or killed.

"Awww, isn't that puppy cute?" Emma leaned out the window and watched the little ball of fur. "Isn't he cute?" she repeated. "Dat, you should absolutely buy us a little puppy like that. He is adorable." She dug into her sweater pocket for her handkerchief, arranged it over her nose, and gave a resounding honk.

Lizzie just couldn't believe it. "Emma, stop blowing your nose so loud. And we don't want a puppy."

Lizzie didn't say more, but she thought to herself how hard it would be to be worried about a puppy just when she was getting used to Snowball. Emma just had no idea how tough it was to be like that. So Lizzie looked out at the brightly colored trees and wished that puppy wouldn't have come running out.

Emma was wiping her nose again. "Do you have a cold or what?" Lizzie asked.

"Of course. Why do you think I'm blowing my nose?" Emma leaned over closer and wiped some more.

The road started to wind steadily upward. Red was breaking into a sweat, so Dat kept him at a walk until they came to a spot where they pulled off beside the road. Red shook his head up and down, so Dat climbed out of the buggy and loosened the rein that was connected to the harness. Red lowered his head and stood patiently while Mam spread the blanket in the soft green grass.

Dat put the picnic basket down and Emma and Lizzie climbed over the front seat. Dat lifted them out, asking if they were hungry.

They all sat together, and ate sandwiches with glasses of cold chocolate milk. Mam spread thick layers of peanut butter on saltine crackers and Lizzie washed hers down with the sweet, creamy chocolate milk. She ate so many crackers that Mam laughed and told her she would turn into a peanut butter girl.

After they had eaten the tart, crunchy apples, Mam packed the leftovers back into the basket while Dat unhitched Red and took him down to the little babbling creek for a drink.

When everyone was back in the buggy, Red pulled them slowly up to the top of the small mountain. They all stopped to rest and look out over the valley, colorful in its autumn splendor. It was a really pretty sight, but Lizzie had eaten too many peanut butter crackers and was getting sleepy. Dat said it was time to turn around and start home, so Lizzie leaned back against the soft cushion and relaxed. Her eyes got heavier as they wound their way down.

Suddenly Lizzie's eyes flew open. They had stopped. Dat was leaning out the door of the buggy and shaking hands with an English man. His wife stood beside him and introduced herself to Mam, who smiled and said hello to her.

As they talked, Lizzie and Emma strained to see out the back window to look at the English couple's home. It was really fancy, with pretty flowers and a swimming pool. Lizzie would have loved to live there and her eyes shone when she told Emma, "Look, they have a swimming pool!"

The English lady spied the little girls, and hurried into the house, returning with three candy bars in her hand.

She oohed and aahed, exclaiming about Emma's rolled hair, and Lizzie watched, hoping Emma wouldn't blow her nose.

After they said goodbye to the friendly couple, Emma looked at her candy bar. Lizzie looked at hers and they asked Mam if they could eat them.

"Of course," Mam said with a smile. "She gave each of you a whole one."

Lizzie carefully unwrapped hers, smelling the delicious chocolate. "Emma, mine has Rice Krispies in it," she said. "Look."

They carefully nibbled on the corner of their candy, and it was so good when it melted on their tongues, Lizzie thought things in Heaven probably tasted like that.

The sun was setting behind the trees as they turned into their driveway. Lizzie was so sleepy and so happy with the lingering taste of that delicious chocolate candy bar still in her mouth, she thought it was the best Sunday in her whole life.

Moving

Lizzie knew something was going on. Something that kept Mam and Dat talking at night, and a man in a long white car came to talk to Dat one afternoon. He had on a brown suit, with a brightly colored yellow tie with a gold clip in it. Dat and the strange man walked around the house, to the harness shop, and even to the barn. The man left soon after he had looked at everything, although he sat at the kitchen table first, talking to both Dat and Mam. He had a stack of papers and Lizzie watched while they both signed their name.

Lizzie understood some of what they were saying, and she thought Dat had to pay the man some money. She knew they talked about money, but it didn't really bother Lizzie much. Emma asked Mam what the man wanted, but Mam told her not to worry about it. Lizzie really looked at Mam because she thought Mam looked sad, and there was a tear in her one eye, she thought.

But Emma wanted to play horse that afternoon and
Lizzie soon forgot about the man in his suit and tie.

Lizzie was not really surprised one morning when
Mam said she wanted to talk to them in the kitchen. She
was baking chocolate chip cookies, and chopping wal-
nuts into tiny pieces as she talked.

"Girls, you know that Dat is not very happy with the
amount of customers he has in the harness shop, don't
you?" she asked.

"Ye-e-s, I guess," Emma said slowly.

"Well, that English man that was here talking to us?"

"Ye-e-s."

"He is a real estate agent, which means he tries to sell
your house for you." Mam watched Lizzie carefully as
she talked, because she knew how sensitive she was.

"Why?" Lizzie bit nervously on her lower lip. "Why
would he want to sell *our* house?"

Mam sighed. "It's kind of a long story, but Dat and
Grandpa Glick found another house in a little town
beside a road that is better traveled and closer to town
for our shop. Besides, it will soon be time to think of
sending you to school, and they said school is only a mile
down the road."

Lizzie's heart felt like it sank way down to her stomach. She felt the tears prick her eyelashes. "I don't want
to go to school," she breathed quietly.

"Not a whole mile away," moaned Emma.

Mam gave the cookie dough a good stir with her long
wooden spoon. She bit her lower lip hard and looked as
if she could cry, but she only took a deep breath.

Lizzie thought it was the saddest moment of her life. The morning sun caught the gleam of the stainless steel teakettle on the gas stove. The white kitchen curtains hung clean and crisp above the sink, where a small vase of flowers stood on the windowsill. She loved the blue and white squares in the linoleum, and Mam's colorful braided rugs placed neatly by the doors and in front of the counter.

How could they just sell this? The little picket fence and the trees in the yard, with the creek rippling and tumbling below the house was just, well, it was home. Lizzie could not imagine living anywhere else.

Mam was plopping spoonfuls of dough on her cookie sheets. She always scraped the dough off with her finger, and patted it into shape, but today her movements were fast and nervous.

"Oh, you will love to go to school, I'm sure. We will live close to other little Amish children your age, and you'll have lots of friends. Our house will seem strange for a while, because the harness shop is on the first floor and we will live on the second floor. That will be exciting—you wait and see."

.   .   .   .   .

So one morning when Lizzie was five years old, a big moving truck pulled up to the little shingled house. Grandpa and Grandma Glick and all the aunts and uncles were there to help load everything onto the truck.

Emma and Lizzie had left early that morning with a driver. Drivers are English people who make a living driving Amish people where they need to go. If the destination is too far away to be traveled by a horse and buggy, or if the town is unsuitable to drive there with a buggy, a van driver is hired.

Lizzie was excited about seeing the new house. She hadn't thought much about it as they helped Mam pack their things carefully in cardboard boxes. But now that they were actually going there, she could hardly wait to see it.

Their hair was freshly combed, with a tight little bob tucked securely with hairpins. Lizzie wore a bright blue dress, and Emma wore her green one. They both had new shoes, because their old ones just weren't suitable to wear anymore—especially if they moved to a new house and all the aunts and uncles came to help.

Lizzie took turns admiring the tops of her new shoes and watching the cornfields and pastures with cows as they zipped along the road. They passed a big farm wagon with two huge workhorses pulling it. She thought those workhorses were really going at a pretty good clip, for as big as they were. Suppose, just suppose, one of them fell? She couldn't imagine how terrible that would be. If the one horse fell down, it would probably pull the other horse down, too. That meant they would stop suddenly and probably the driver would go flying off the wagon. Surely he would die, or at least go to the hospital with all his arms and legs broken. It was too awful to think about.

The driver slowed down, turning into a short driveway, and there was the house. Lizzie looked up and up. It was so huge and so white, she could not imagine living up so far. She bit her lower lip and stared at that huge white house.

"Come, Lizzie! Come on!" Emma was already jumping out of the van. Mam and Mandy were standing in the yard, and Mam was paying the driver, and smiling and talking to the aunts. So there was nothing for Lizzie to do but jump down after Emma and see what it looked like inside.

First Aunt Bertha caught them both by the hand. "Hey, how are my girls? All ready to explore this big new house?"

Emma giggled. "Hi, Aunt Bertha!"

Lizzie smiled up at her. "Yes, we can hardly wait!"

"You just be careful you don't fall down those stairs! Do you know you have to go up and down every time you want to go somewhere?" she asked.

Emma shrugged her shoulders. "Oh, well."

But Lizzie looked long and hard at those stairs and sincerely hoped she wouldn't fall. She'd be very careful.

Upstairs, the house was a bit old. Lizzie didn't think it was as pretty as their little shingled house, but it was alright. Everywhere she looked, someone was carrying something or unpacking a box, or cleaning windows. It was all so confusing. Lizzie couldn't make any sense of it. So she stood against the wall and watched, wishing everyone would finish up and leave.

The kitchen had wooden cupboards that were brown and not as bright-looking as the white ones Lizzie was used to. The linoleum was reddish-brown and cracked in some places. But when the men brought Mam's china cupboard, it seemed a little bit like home.

Emma opened a door off to the left and found the bathroom. Lizzie tried the water faucet, and—sure enough—the water gushed out and down the drain. They found a strange-looking little cupboard hanging above the sink, which was actually a mirror on the outside.

The bathtub was so huge, they both had a case of the giggles. Emma said it was almost like a swimming pool, and Lizzie told her they were going to fill it almost to the top to see if they could really swim in it.

Aunt Bertha came through the doorway with a huge box marked "Bathroom." She shooed them out, saying there was no room in that small bathroom for that big box, herself, and both of them. Lizzie turned around

outside the bathroom door and made a face, saying quietly to Emma, "Bossy old thing."

From there they made their way between boxes,
crumpled newspapers, things strewn all over the floor,
and fussy aunts in every corner doing something, until
they found Mam. She was stirring a big stainless steel
kettle of soup that smelled so good it made Lizzie's stomach growl.

"Mam, I'm really hungry." Lizzie laid her head against
Mam's stomach, and Mam reached down to touch
Lizzie's cheek. The touch was reassuring—so much that
she thought wherever Mam was cooking good food, that
was home to her.

"Dinner's almost ready. Lizzie, why don't you go find
Dat and tell him to bring the men for dinner?"

So Emma and Lizzie found the stairs, and went across
a long narrow porch until they heard men's voices in
the back yard. There were apples lying in the grass, so
they supposed those trees must be apple trees. The grass
needed mowing badly, and Lizzie wondered how Dat
was ever going to push the mower through that tall,
thick grass.

Dat was unloading hay in the barn across the driveway. Uncle James was helping and they were talking
and laughing. Dat looked as if he thought this was exciting, so Lizzie thought he must enjoy moving into a new
home.

"Dat!" Emma called.

He spied the girls and a big smile crossed his face.
His gray eyes shone at them and he said, "There are my

girls! Did you move along with us to our new house? I
thought we left you back at the other place!"

Lizzie ran over to him and slipped her hand into his.
"Dat, you know me and Emma came with the driver.
Mam and Mandy did, too."

Dat squeezed her hand, smiling down at her and said,
"Of course you did. If you were still back at the other
house, I would go get you right now with a driver."

Emma took his other hand and said, "Dat, Mam said
dinner is ready now."

Uncle James said, "Hello, Emma and Lizzie!"

"Hello," they echoed shyly. They knew Uncle James,
but they didn't see him very often, so they were shy. He
was tall and dark-haired, with black eyes that smiled
and twinkled easily.

"Did you say dinner is ready?" he asked.

"Yes," Emma answered. "Mam said to come now."

"Alright-y, here we go," Dat sang out. He told the
other men to go along, and they all trooped up the stairs
to the kitchen where Mam was setting the soup and beef
barbeque on the table.

After they had bowed their heads in silent prayer,
they ate wherever they could find room to sit.

Grandma Glick fixed Emma's plate, while Aunt Sarah
helped Lizzie. They set their bowls of steaming hot
chicken-corn-noodle soup on an upside-down cardboard
box, and brought a drink for them.

Lizzie crumbled saltine crackers into her soup, stirred
it, and took a big bite. Pain exploded on her tongue and
she leaned forward, letting the whole mouthful fall back
into her bowl.

"Ouch! Watch it, Emma! That soup is too hot." Lizzie took a long drink of cold water, letting her tongue stay in the cool water after she was finished. Emma was shaking her head, trying to cool her mouthful of soup. They took big bites of their beef barbeque sandwiches, and ate cold, crisp little sweet pickles and slices of white cheese.

For dessert, Grandma Glick had made a chocolate cake, covered with thick, creamy caramel frosting. Aunt Sally brought golden yellow vanilla cornstarch pudding, and Lizzie piled great spoonfuls of it on top of her chocolate cake. It squished into her cheeks as she chewed, and the sugary frosting stuck to her teeth. It was so delicious, Emma amd Lizzie agreed it was the best thing they had ever tasted.

After dinner, Aunt Sally told the girls she was getting their room ready. If they wanted to, they could come help her and arrange their own things on their dresser.

Lizzie thought she wanted to be exactly like Aunt Sally when she grew older. She was thin, but not too thin, and her hair had little waves in it. If she didn't wet it before making her bob, she wouldn't look much like an Amish girl. And she had a real boyfriend. Lizzie had seen him once, driving past their house in his open buggy. Young boys had buggies with no roof or windows, and they were actually only for the young people.

Lizzie wished she was Aunt Sally, having ripply hair, a boyfriend, and going away in a buggy without a roof.

Aunt Sally put the little dresser scarf on the dresser, and Emma arranged their things. Lizzie just let her do it, because Aunt Sally was there. But that was the thing about Emma. She was so bossy. Just because she was the oldest, didn't mean she could always tell Lizzie what to do.

After they were finished and Aunt Sally had carefully scrubbed the wooden floor with a clean-smelling bucket of soapy water, Lizzie lay down on her bed. The pink chenille bedspread felt soft to her cheek, and her favorite teddy bear smiled at her from her dresser. The pink curtains at the window shone in the afternoon sun, and Emma's green dress made everything look brighter. She was on her knees, arranging everything in perfect order in her drawers.

That was another thing about Emma. She was so particular, so fussy about everything. She always hung up her dress on the little rack, put her bedroom slippers side by side under the bed, and brushed her teeth for a very long time in the evening.

Lizzie almost never hung up her clothes and tried hard to get away without brushing her teeth. Emma always yelled for Mam, so Lizzie usually brushed her teeth rebelliously.

Then, Emma always knelt beside her bed and said her prayers with bowed head and clasped hands, her dark head bowed in sincere devotion. Lizzie said her prayers, too, but just because Emma did, and Mam taught them to do it. She always wondered if there was any use.

Her eyes got heavier and heavier, and amid the hustle and bustle of moving day, she fell sound asleep. She didn't know Emma covered her carefully with a blanket and tiptoed out, closing the door behind her.

The New Pony

Today Emma and Lizzie were going with Dat. He was going to a horse auction in a faraway town, with a driver. Uncle James and a friend who lived close to the Glicks were also going.

Lizzie had never been to a horse auction. Emma said there were a hundred horses there, but Lizzie guessed there were more than that. They asked Dat and he said there were not a thousand, but maybe more than a hundred.

Mam combed their hair, and they brushed their teeth till they shone. They decided to both wear blue dresses, and after they had on their new shoes, Lizzie felt pretty. She didn't really know if she was. She just loved to watch the toes of her new shoes, because they made her feel nice. She wondered if she would ever get to wear high heels.

Mam was getting Mandy ready, too. Mam was happy
this morning, because she had made a new friend who
lived just across the street. She was thin and had the
prettiest red hair Lizzie had ever seen. Her name was
Evelyn and she was a Mennonite. She wore a small covering, drove a black car, and they had electricity in their
house. Mom and Evelyn soon became good friends, and
this morning they were going to buy groceries and do
some other shopping.

Lizzie sometimes felt sad when Mam wasn't happy, so
she was glad to see Mam go shopping with Evelyn.

Dat was closing up the shop downstairs. The harness
shop was all set up now, and Dat worked long hours
because of more orders. The saddle tree was filled with
shiny black and brown saddles. The Coca-Cola cooler
stood in the corner, and the walls were lined with wood-
en shelves. All kinds of shoes and boots were stocked on
these shelves. Lizzie waited impatiently till Dat came up
the stairs and into the kitchen.

"Dat, when is our driver coming? I was ready for a
long, long time. Soon my dress is going to be all wrinkled if we don't soon leave," Lizzie complained.

Mam said, "You'll be going soon, Lizzie." She was
watching across the street and told them all to have a
nice time. It was time for her to go shopping with Evelyn.

Lizzie sighed. She watched out the window and
wished the driver would come. Emma told her to settle
down and stop being so fidgety because it made her
nervous.

Just when Lizzie thought she couldn't wait one second longer, a noisy honk made her eyes fly open and she jumped straight off the couch.

"He's here! Emma, come on, the driver's here!"

Emma jumped up, and they ran to the door. "Dat, are you ready?" Emma yelled.

"Let's go!" Lizzie hopped up and down.

Dat laughed at them and together they hurried out the door to the waiting vehicle.

As they wound their way along the country roads, Lizzie just knew this was going to be a special day. For one thing, she had never seen a horse auction, and she loved horses. And she was almost sure Dat was going to buy their lunch at a restaurant, or maybe just at a food stand. She hoped so much Dat would buy french fries. That was the best food in the world besides chocolate cake and vanilla pudding.

"Lizzie! Oh, I mean it—look!" Emma was peering out the window on her side.

Lizzie scooted over and stared. There were lots of cars, trucks, horses, ponies, and people, all milling around beside a huge yellow and white tent. There were men wearing white cowboy hats, and even women wearing them.

The driver found a parking space and Dat hopped out, telling the girls to stay with him, because they were going to look at the ponies first.

Lizzie just looked and looked. She had to blink her eyes in the bright sunlight, but she squinted them and kept on looking. The ponies were tied away from the big horses. There were big black ponies, little woolly brown ones, white skinny ones, and little fat ponies. Lizzie wanted every one. She tried to stay with Dat, but she had to stay and stroke the satiny ears of the little brown one.

"Dat, are you going to buy us one?" Lizzie looked imploringly at Dat. "Is that why we came here?"

Dat smiled down at the girls and his eyes twinkled. "Oh, I thought maybe I would ask two little girls if they really wanted a pony, but then I thought, what would they want with a pony if we don't have a cart? And what about a harness?"

Emma slapped his pant leg, and Lizzie just hopped up and down till she thought she would burst with excitement.

"Dat! Why would you worry about a harness? You know you can make a good pony harness for us!" Emma emphatically nodded her head up and down.

So they walked among the ponies and Dat looked at them all. His eyes were still twinkling, but he didn't say much.

Lizzie was walking along the rows of ponies when a warm little nose touched her arm. She jumped and turned, coming face to face with the softest dark gray eyes. The pony's head was gray and white, and his forelocks hung down over his soft gray eyes. Lizzie was so amazed, she just stood and gazed at this pretty pony, and the pony gazed back at Lizzie. The pony reached out and nibbled softly on her little black apron.

Softly, almost as if in a dream, Lizzie reached out

one hand and touched the coarse hair of the pony's forelocks. The pony gently put his head down against Lizzie's soft stomach, while she slowly stroked his head.

Lizzie didn't know a pony's hair could be so soft. She loved that pony so much, she thought she couldn't stand it if Dat couldn't buy him. "Hello, little horse. My little horse," she whispered in awe. "How are you doing?"

The little gray pony stood by Lizzie, and laid his head against her. Lizzie reached back farther and stroked his neck, and looked at the color of the pony. He was so pretty, all different colors in little circles, white, gray, and darker gray. His tail hung on the ground, it was so long. Lizzie stayed there with the gray pony, forgetting all about Dat and Emma.

Suddenly a man's voice boomed across the loudspeaker and the crowd moved slowly toward it. The auction was starting! Lizzie gave the pony a final pat and turned to talk to Dat and Emma. They were not there. Actually, Lizzie couldn't see them anywhere. She looked left, then right, but could only see English people she didn't know. Her heart beat faster. She started walking swiftly and she called in a very small voice, "Dat!" She just couldn't see anyone she knew, and fear gripped her heart as she started to run. Tears pricked at her eyelashes and her voice shook as she called louder, "Dat! Emma!"

Nobody answered, so Lizzie stood in the middle of the crowd and put her face in her little black apron and cried. Sobs tore at her throat and hot tears poured down her cheeks.

"Hey! Hey! What have we here? What's wrong, little

one?" A huge white cowboy hat, with a darkly tanned face with piercing blue eyes was down at Lizzie's level as the cowboy hunkered down in front of her.

Lizzie was scared and so embarrassed, but she peeped over the safety of her apron and sniffed.

"Did you lose your dad, little girl?" He smiled kindly at her, and Lizzie thought his teeth grew from his mustache.

"Ya," Lizzie nodded her head.

"Ya?" He laughed, and straightened up, taking her trembling little hand. "I guess that means 'yes'."

"Yes. I cannot find him," Lizzie replied in her best English manners.

He smiled down at her and said, "I think I know who your dad is. Do you have another sister?"

Lizzie nodded her head again.

"Okay, then, here we go." And he pushed through the crowd, holding her hand safely in his.

"Lizzie!" Dat came hurrying through the crowd. "Thank the Lord someone found you!"

Emma ran up to Lizzie, holding her hand firmly. Dat told the cowboy he was very grateful to him for bringing his daughter back.

"She must've been

with the ponies too long, huh?" he asked Lizzie.

Lizzie smiled shyly through the last of her tears, and Emma got her handkerchief and wiped Lizzie's face, just like a little mother. Lizzie was so glad to see Emma, she didn't even care if she acted bossy.

Dat and the cowboy talked a while longer, then he told the girls goodbye. "You'd better stay with your dad and sister, little one," he told her, patting her head.

"Tell him thank you, Lizzie," Dat said.

"Thank you," Lizzie said quietly.

"Be good, sweetheart," the cowboy said with a smile, and he walked slowly away, his boots making a dull, clapping sound.

Dat asked Lizzie quite seriously what happened that they became separated. Lizzie told him about the gray pony and how much she wanted that one.

"But, Dat, do you think you'll have enough money?" She stood on her tiptoes, twisting her black apron in her fingers. Her eyes were so anxious, and she looked so pale, Dat's heart was touched. *That's my Lizzie,* he thought. *When she wants something, she really, really wants it.*

When it was time for the ponies to be sold, in the very front row stood Dat, with Emma and a very anxious little Lizzie.

As the bidding started, and the first pony was led into the ring, Lizzie's knees began to shake. Her teeth chattered, and she clenched the iron rail in front of her. She looked nervously over at Emma, who stood calmly watching the people and chewing her gum.

Lizzie tried hard to stop her teeth from chattering, but

the auctioneer's singsong voice gave her goose bumps.
So her teeth chattered even more, and just when she
thought she couldn't take one more minute of suspense,
the gray pony was led to the ring.

"D-d-dat!" Lizzie tried to talk but she just pointed
instead.

"That one?" Dat asked.

Lizzie only nodded her head yes, looking wildly at
Dat with huge, terrified eyes.

The auctioneer told the crowd about this nice little
gray mare, how old she was, and that she was broke to
drive or ride. Lizzie understood some of it, but she only
knew that never in her life had she wished so hard for
something.

The auctioneer kept going, and Dat kept nodding
his head. Lizzie's heart beat loudly in her ears, and her
cheeks hurt from biting down on her chattering teeth.
Suddenly Dat held up a card with big black numbers on
it and he let out a loud breath.

"She's ours, girls—we bought her!" he told them.

Lizzie beamed and beamed. She laughed out loud,
and skipped only a little bit, because people were watching them. As they made their way through the crowd,
Lizzie found Emma's hand and squeezed. "Emma, we
have a pony," she breathed.

"It's a girl pony, even. She's so pretty. We're going to
drive her and ride her and feed her apples," Emma said.

"Yep!" Lizzie hopped on one foot. "Hey! And we
have all those apples in our yard!"

Emma frowned. "But, Lizzie, you can't give our pony

too many apples or she'll get sick. Just one or two."

Lizzie was too happy to even think Emma was bossy, so she just agreed nicely.

So later that evening, in their little barn in the back yard, the Glick family all worked together, spreading fresh straw and building a little wooden trough for the pony's oats. Lizzie ran in circles and swept the floor wherever Emma hadn't swept.

And when a trailer pulled in the drive, and a small gray pony found a new home, Lizzie's world was full to overflowing with happy thoughts.

School

Emma and Lizzie stood on the porch, their hair freshly done, and wearing brand new lavender dresses with black aprons. Their new shoes were not brand spanking new anymore, but they still looked very nice.

Emma clutched a little metal lunchbox in her hand. Lizzie held one exactly like Emma's, except Mam had tied a piece of red yarn on the handle, so Lizzie would know which one was hers.

It was the first day of school. Emma was six years old now, but Lizzie was only five. Actually, Lizzie was almost too young to go, but Mam wanted them to start together. They were only a little over a year apart in age, so it was good to start their first grade the same year.

They were waiting on the neighbor girl who they were supposed to walk to school with. She was a lot older, and her name was Lavina Lapp. The girls had met

her since living in their new house above the harness
shop, and she was always friendly and talkative. Lizzie
liked her.

"Here she comes," Emma breathed nervously.

"Does she?" Lizzie looked around for Mam and
Mandy, but they had gone back upstairs. She dashed
to the door of the harness shop and yelled, "Dat! We're
leaving now! Goodbye, Dat!"

His head appeared around the saddle tree. "Oh,
Lizzie—are you going now? Be good girls, and I'll see
you this afternoon."

"Bye, Dat," they called in unison.

"Bye, girls," Mam waved from the kitchen window.

"Bye, Mam!" They turned their eager faces up to the
kitchen window as they waved to Mandy. Lizzie wasn't
sure, but she thought it looked like Mam wiped away a
tear. Lizzie felt a lump rise in her throat, but she soon
felt better when Lavina Lapp smiled at her.

"Good morning," she said.

"Hi!" Emma said brightly.

"All ready? Good, let's go, because we don't want to
be late the first morning,
do we?"

So they started up
the road at a brisk
walk. Lizzie was too
excited to think
about getting
tired. Lavina
Lapp chattered

on about school, and Emma walked beside her, answering her questions and asking some of her own. Lizzie didn't say much. She just kept walking and was careful to get off the road when a vehicle passed.

They passed a farm, cornfields where heavy ears of corn hung on brown stalks, and a herd of black and white cows grazing.

The little white one-room schoolhouse came into view, and Lizzie's heart did a complete flip-flop. There was a porch, and a fence with a gate that was pulled open. A horse shed and two outdoor bathrooms stood in a corner of the school yard. There were already lots of children at school and Lizzie felt very afraid.

She bit down hard on her lower lip and watched the children as they walked through the gate. Some of the boys were throwing a baseball, but others turned to stare at them. Lizzie just kept walking, clutching her lunchbox tighter in her hand.

"Good morning!" The teacher stood on the porch, watching them approach. Lizzie hid behind Lavina as she said, "Good morning," to the teacher.

Emma said, "Good morning," too, but not very loud. Lizzie didn't say anything. She just stared at the teacher. She was very thin, with a long black dress. Her forehead was wide, and she wore glasses, and her white covering was bigger than Mam's. She looked friendly enough, but she also looked scary. Lizzie wondered if she spanked little first graders. She looked like she could really spank.

The teacher bent down and smiled at Lizzie. "So, you

must be Emma Glick's sister? Is it Lizzie?"

Lizzie nodded her head yes. She looked up at the teacher's face and tried to smile, although her mouth was shaking a bit.

"So you are both in the first grade this year? And Lizzie, you are not quite six years old yet. Do you think you will be able to pull your share?" She smiled at Lizzie and continued, "My name is Sylvia King. But you may call me Teacher, or Teacher Sylvia."

They turned to enter the schoolroom, and Lizzie opened her eyes wide in astonishment. She had never seen a blackboard of that size. It was huge and black, with rows of letters on a white board above it. In front of the blackboard stood the teacher's desk, with a neat row of books stacked on top. Beside the desk was a shiny brown coal stove, with a stainless steel teakettle on top and a hod of coal beside it. The walls were painted a pale blue color, with white blinds hanging at the windows. But the most amazing thing was the row after row of wooden desks. The sides were black wrought iron, and each desktop had a small hole on top, with a crease to hold your pencil.

Lizzie walked shyly over to the first desk and touched it. She felt the crease along the top and wondered what the hole was for.

Along the back wall were rows of bright gold hooks mounted on pale brown boards. There was a piece of adhesive tape above every hook, with names written in black letters. Lizzie wondered if her name was anywhere, but it was too far to walk by herself. She felt safer to stay against the big desk, close to Emma.

Teacher Sylvia walked to the back of the room and pulled on a long rope that disappeared into a small hole in the ceiling. Lizzie heard the sound of those wonderful bells for the very first time. She never tired of the deep, "dong-dong" sound after that.

Suddenly, a herd of children, all ages, sizes, and descriptions, burst through the door. Their metal lunchboxes clattered as they set them on the low wooden shelf. Lizzie looked down at hers, still clenched tightly in her hand. She punched Emma in the ribs and whispered, "Aren't you going to put your lunch away?"

"Oh." Emma looked as scared as Lizzie felt. "I guess. Come with me."

Lizzie marched bravely after Emma and they put their lunches on an empty shelf. They watched as the other children looked on the top of every desk. Emma whispered to Lizzie to just stay with her. Teacher Sylvia came to the back of the room and put her hand on Lizzie's shoulder.

"Come, girls, we'll find your seats. You'll find your name written on the piece of tape. Let's see if you can find your seats. Can you write your own name?"

Emma nodded her head. Lizzie was too shy to do anything except walk along under that hand on her shoulder. It seemed so far across the classroom and she felt like every pair of eyes was staring at her. She hoped her dress was buttoned properly and her bob was not falling down.

"Here we are—first grade," Teacher Sylvia said.

Lizzie looked around and saw two small girls and a boy who also looked a bit shaken. They all found their desks and slid into them, sneaking shy glances at each other.

Lizzie's desk was the first one before the teacher's desk. When Teacher Sylvia sat down, Lizzie was really close to her. It was comforting to know the teacher was nearby, and this way she could easily see the blackboard.

She squirmed a little to make herself more comfortable on the slippery varnished seat. She tucked her legs underneath, and her new shoes crinkled at the toes. She laid her arms on the desk, and clasped her hands together. She sighed a little, trying to relax enough to listen to what Teacher Sylvia was saying.

First she said loudly and clearly, "Good morning, boys and girls!"

Most of the children answered, "Good morning, Teacher." Some of the little ones didn't say it at all, and others whispered it shyly. But everyone kind of said it all together, so you couldn't really tell.

After that, the teacher started reading from the Bible in her loud, clear voice. Lizzie tried to follow carefully, but she kept stealing glances at the girl beside her.

She was about the same size as Lizzie, and she was wearing a dark green dress that had little bumps in it. Lizzie wished her lavender dress was as fancy as hers.

Now the teacher closed the Bible and they all rose and stood beside their desks. They all said the Lord's Prayer, except Lizzie and Emma didn't know it, so they just stood quietly and listened.

After the prayer was finished, they took turns to file
to the front of the room. Lizzie didn't know how they
could all know what to do, because the teacher didn't
tell them.

She stood by the blackboard and turned some stu-
dents around, or changed the taller ones with some who
were shorter. Lizzie and Emma were put in the front
row, where all the little children stood. Lizzie wished
she could see behind her, but she was much too shy. So
she just blinked her eyes and tried to stand up straight
beside Emma.

Teacher Sylvia handed out blue songbooks to some of
the children. Lizzie wondered why they didn't all have
one until the teacher showed them how to share. She
smiled and said, "Now we're going to take turns to pick
a song. Elam, you are the first one in the back row, so
you may pick first."

There was an awkward pause, and some of the first
graders did turn around to see who Elam was, but Lizzie
kept looking straight ahead because she wanted to be a
good girl on the first day of school.

A voice from the back announced, "Forty-eight,"
and everyone noisily flipped through the pages of the
songbook. Lizzie and Emma didn't know how to find
that page, so they just stood there. Lizzie felt scared and
very, very lonely. She swallowed and tried not to feel so
sad, but it welled up until tears pricked her eyes.

Teacher Sylvia walked over and helped Lizzie find the
page. The singing welled around them louder and loud-

er, and Lizzie bit her lip, trying hard not to feel lonely.

> *"My Lord, what a morning,*
> *My Lord, what a morning,*
> *My Lord, what a morning,*
> *When the stars begin to fall."*

On and on the children sang, and lonelier and lonelier Lizzie became. She tried to think of happy things, of good things to eat, and of silly things, but the huge lump in her throat only grew bigger. She looked down and bit her lip, shuffling her feet, but the lump in her throat would not go away. She glanced at Emma, and Emma smiled a weak smile, trying to cheer her up.

In that moment, huge, wet tears coursed down Lizzie's cheeks, and a harsh sob escaped her bitten lips. She was soon crying uncontrollably, wishing she could go home to Mam before the stars fell and the end of the world came. Wouldn't it be awful, if the stars fell from the sky and she was in school, and Dat and Mam were at home?

Emma touched her arm, and Teacher Sylvia put her hand on her shoulder. Lizzie cast a terrified glance at the teacher, but she was whispering to Emma.

Emma took Lizzie's hand and tugged gently. Lizzie followed Emma across that big expanse of schoolroom to the door while the singing went on. Emma led her across the porch and down to the little outdoor bathroom. They huddled together while Emma tried to console Lizzie in earnest tones.

"Lizzie, it's okay. What's wrong?"

Lizzie cried horribly. She couldn't tell Emma about

the deep black loneliness she felt when they sang that song. So she just shrugged her shoulders, and Emma wiped her eyes and told her to be quiet. She said Lizzie would have to be a good girl and grow up now, and not cry in school. So Lizzie gulped and choked and nodded her head. She would be all right, she assured Emma. And much to Lizzie's surprise, she really was.

And she learned to love school, in spite of sad songs.

Going for Milk

One afternoon when the girls came home from school, Mam had made fresh molasses cookies, and the smell of the kitchen was warm and cozy after the wind blew them home.

The cookies were all in rows on a blue tablecloth. They were dark brown in color, and little cracks ran across the top. Crystal white sugar was sprinkled over them, and some fell into the little "ditches." Lizzie loved molasses cookies, especially when Mam made hot cocoa to dip them in.

Mandy came running to greet them, and Lizzie threw her lunchbox on the counter and hugged her. "Hi, Mandy!"

Mandy squealed with delight and hugged Lizzie back. "Hi, Lizzie!"

"What did you do today?" asked Lizzie.

"Made cookies," Mandy told her proudly. "I helped put sugar on them."

Mam went to the refrigerator to get milk to make cocoa. She rearranged a few pitchers and said, "Oh, no—we're completely out of milk!"

Emma already had her mouth full of cookie. "Mmmm," she mumbled.

"I know." Lizzie hopped up and down. "We'll go! We'll hitch up Dolly and go to Uncle James's for milk. We could, easy!"

Mam looked a bit doubtful, but when Emma chimed in, she got the little tin gallon jug ready for them.

"Alright, then. But you have to ask Dat to help you hitch up. Emma, you know you have to go the back alley, and don't even think of going on the road."

"We won't, we won't!"

The girls dashed down the stairs and burst into the harness shop. Dat looked up from his sewing machine. He never had a chance to say hello or smile before the girls yelled, "Dat, Mam said if you help us hitch up Dolly we're allowed to go to Uncle James's for milk. Are you going to?"

Dat put down his piece of leather and swiveled in his stool. He took his pipe from his mouth and set it beside the sewing machine. He got up and smiled down at them.

"Are you sure Mam said it's alright?"

"Yep, she did," Lizzie said, a bit carefully, because she was so afraid he'd say no.

But he didn't. His eyes twinkled, and he took Emma's

hand. "Alright. I'll help you hitch up. You know you have to stay on the back alley, don't you?"

"Sure, sure. Mam said so, too," Emma assured him. "We promise," Lizzie added.

When they came to the barn, Dat opened the big doors where the pony cart was kept. The big buggy was in there, too. The cart was little, a lot smaller than the buggy, and had only two wheels. Dat had painted it with thick, glossy black paint and very carefully drew gold lines down the shafts and around the seat. It was actually a very fancy cart and Lizzie was so glad Dad liked fancy pony carts. She thought it was the prettiest thing she had ever seen, besides high-heeled shoes at the store.

Emma opened the gate to Dolly's pen and led her out. They never tired of looking at Dolly. She was often brushed and cared for lovingly. They fed her carrots and so many apples that fell from the tree in the yard that Dolly got sick. So Dat told them they were not allowed to give her any more apples until she felt better.

Emma brushed Dolly, and Lizzie just stroked her smooth, satiny neck. Dat watched while Emma carefully brushed across Dolly's rump. "Always stand to the side, Emma. If you stand right behind a horse or pony, they could be frightened and kick you," he told her.

"Oh, I know that, Dat," Emma answered airily. Lizzie chimed in, "You already did tell us that lots of times."

Dat smiled. "Oh," was all he said, and there was a smile on his face.

When Emma grabbed the little black pony harness and slung it across Dolly's back, he smiled some more.

These little girls certainly shared his love of ponies, he
thought. He watched as Lizzie raced to the other side
to fasten the crupper that went under Dolly's tail. She
stood carefully to the side as he had taught them. Dat
handed the bridle to Lizzie, and watched as she tried
to put the bit between Dolly's teeth. Dolly would not
open her mouth. Lizzie kept tugging the bit, and saying,
"C'mon Dolly—open your mouth!"

Dat showed Lizzie how to put her finger along the
back of Dolly's mouth and press in. Nothing happened.
Dolly just wouldn't open her mouth. So Dat put his
hand under the pony's jaw, pressed along the back,
and—just like magic—Dolly popped her mouth open.
Lizzie quickly slipped in the bit, and they pulled the
bridle up over the ears, fastening the chin strap along
the side of the pony's face.

The bridle had two big black pieces of stiff leather
on each side of Dolly's head. That was so she couldn't
see what was beside or behind her. Lizzie often thought
about blinders—that's what they were called. And she
thought they were very cruel. If she was a horse, she
wouldn't do it to wear them. Sometimes when Lizzie
was running, she put her hands on each side of her head
and thought how awful that would be for the horses.

But she didn't think about that now, as they pulled
the pony cart up to Dolly and put the shafts into the
leather loops that supported them. Lizzie pulled one
thick strap from Dolly's back and fastened it to the cart.
Emma did the same on the other side. Then they clipped
the snap from the leather wound around the shafts to

the britchment, and they were all set. Dad unwound the leather reins and watched as the girls clambered into the cart. Emma set the tin milk jug carefully in one corner on the floor, and Dat handed her the reins.

Emma grasped them firmly in both hands, smiled at Dat, and said, "We'll be back soon. Bye!"

"Bye!" Lizzie waved happily as Emma clicked her tongue.

Dat stepped back and waved as Dolly started off. They had to make a circle, so they could go behind the barn, where a narrow alley ran along the back yards of the neighbors' houses.

Dolly trotted along, and they passed backyard fences, gardens, and doghouses. Mrs. Zimmerman was hanging out her dishtowels on a small line on the porch, and she waved at Emma and Lizzie. They waved back.

Lizzie felt so important, with only her and Emma sitting on that pony cart seat. She thought Mrs. Zimmerman probably thought they looked cute. Lizzie felt cute.

They came to Uncle James's lane, and Emma carefully stopped Dolly by pulling back on the reins.

"Whoa, Dolly," she called.

Dolly stopped and they looked both ways to see if there was a car coming. There wasn't, of course, but you never knew when a car would pull into Uncle James's lane. Emma pulled gently on one rein and clicked her tongue; Dolly stepped out obediently.

Lizzie was so filled with love for this nice pony. She sighed and told Emma they had the best pony in the whole world.

"I know," Emma agreed. "She just listens so well and

not just that, Lizzie—we're pretty little to be driving this pony all by ourselves."

"Then yet, we have to get milk," Lizzie agreed. She sat up straighter and pulled in her stomach. "I think we are actually grown-up for our age."

Dolly trotted along, and the breeze rippled the grass by the side of the lane. As they approached the buildings, they saw Uncle James in the cornfield picking corn with two huge workhorses. He waved at the girls and they waved back as hard as they could.

They drove around the big white barn and pulled up to the hitching rack. There was a chain-link fence around their yard, and a gate that opened into it. A sidewalk led up to the porch of the old stone house. Everything was mowed and trimmed to perfection. There were a few leaves in the yard, and a few more bright yellow ones fell to the ground. Lizzie thought Aunt Becca would probably rake them soon.

"Lizzie, you go ask Aunt Becca for milk, and I'll stay here and watch Dolly, okay?" Emma asked.

"Why don't you tie her?" Lizzie wondered.

"I forgot a neck rope," Emma answered.

"Oh." Lizzie looked around. "You could use the chain that hangs down there," Lizzie pointed.

"I guess I could," Emma said. She hopped off the cart, grabbed the chain, and clipped the bright silver snap to the ring in Dolly's bit.

They both jumped when Aunt Becca came up behind the cart and said, "Well, girls! What are you doing? Driving that pony all by yourself, Emma? My, you must

really be brave today!" She smiled at them as she picked
up the reins from the ground. "Here. You should always
put the reins through this ring when you tie your pony."

Lizzie loved Aunt Becca. She was short and often
wore a navy bandanna on her head, with a knot under
her bob. She was always working hard and usually singing or whistling. She had only one little baby daughter,
whose name was Arie, and her house was so clean that
the linoleum shone like a mirror.

"We need this filled with milk," Emma said, as she
handed the jug to Aunt Becca.

"Alright-y," she said, as she started toward the milkhouse. "Come along."

The girls trotted along as Aunt Becca walked rapidly toward the barn. Inside the milkhouse there was
a huge stainless steel tank filled with rich, foamy milk.
Aunt Becca yanked open one side of the lid on the tank
and lowered a clean stainless steel dipper into the vast
amount of milk. A few turns of her wrist and the tin jug
was filled to the brim. She fastened the top, closed the
tank lid, and rinsed the dipper and jug under running
water in a huge stainless steel rinse tub.

"There you go, girls," she smiled. "I'll just write this
down, then when your Dat comes to settle up at the end
of the month, he'll pay for it."

"Is Arie sleeping?" Emma asked.

"Yes, she is finally taking a good nap," Aunt Becca
sighed.

"Was she grouchy today?" Lizzie asked.

Aunt Becca laughed. "Yes, I guess you could say she

was grouchy today. But she's teething, so she's in pain, too. What I need is two little girls like you to help me babysit while I help Uncle James in the field."

Emma looked at her seriously. "We could."

Lizzie wished Emma wouldn't say that. She often felt bad, but she really didn't like babies that much. Especially if they yelled and screamed, and drooled on your hand if you held them. In church, all the little girls wanted to get someone's baby after services, so they could play they were the mother. Lizzie never liked that. Babies were just such a mess, and they made Lizzie nervous.

So when Aunt Becca said, "No, I was only kidding," Lizzie was immensly relieved. She even gave Aunt Becca an extra-big smile as they loosened the snap and picked up the reins. The jug of milk was put securely in the box, and they were ready to go.

"Thank you!" They waved and smiled as Dolly trotted out the lane. Aunt Becca watched and then turned to get her rake.

"Emma, why did you say we could babysit for Arie?" Lizzie asked her sourly.

"Why?"

"Because."

"Well, what's wrong with that?" Emma wanted to know.

"Oh, nothing." Lizzie wasn't going to tell Emma that she didn't like babies very much, because Emma would think there was something wrong with her. So they drove on in silence. Emma guessed Lizzie was just grouchy because she was not allowed to be the driver. Dat said she had to wait until she was older, and Lizzie was that way. She never really gave up right.

They turned off the lane and headed up the alley. Suddenly a fierce barking broke the silence. A huge black and brown German Shepherd dog lunged at Dolly's heels. Up, up came Dolly's head, until it looked like her back was straight up and she would topple over backward.

Everything was just a horrible blur as they strove to stay on the seat. The reins were loose, so Dolly reared in terror. The dog's harsh barking terrified Lizzie as much as Dolly.

Dolly jerked as she hit the ground running, and Lizzie and Emma were thrown onto the hard gravel.

Lizzie felt a blow to her backside, and her head slammed against the hard earth. Stars exploded in her head, as she yelled as loud as she could. It hurt so much, she just kept screaming. When her sight cleared, she saw Emma sitting in the grass, crying with all her might. The tin jug of milk was lying on its side, and milk was splattered every-where.

Way in the distance, she saw Dolly galloping home
with the empty cart bouncing behind her. The reins
were flapping loosely on the ground as she rounded the
corner to the barn.

Emma picked herself up and came over to Lizzie.
"Lizzie, stop screaming!" she cried. She jerked back at
the sight of all the blood in Lizzie's hair.

"Ewww, Lizzie—your head! It's all bloody! Lizzie, I
hope you're not going to die!" And Emma cried harder
than ever.

Lizzie felt her head, and terror welled up anew. Her
fingers were red and sticky with blood, and she gazed at
them in disbelief. The only thing she could do now was
sit there and cry along with Emma.

That is how Dat and Mam found their girls. After
seeing Dolly come running home with an empty cart,
Mam's knees turned weak with fear. She ran into the
harness shop and called for Dat. With great fear, they
both ran down the alley, praying their little girls would
not be seriously hurt.

As they approached, Mam was relieved to hear
their cries. At least they were conscious. Dat reached
them first, and fell on his knees beside Emma. "Emma,
Emma!" was all he could manage, as he felt all over to
make sure she was alright.

He ran over to Lizzie, where Mam was kneeling and
had found the wound in her head. "My poor baby. Poor
Lizzie," she crooned, as she cradled her in her warm, comforting arms. Emma came over and stood in the safe haven
of Dat's arms as Mam finished examining Lizzie's wound.

"It's not too deep," she said softly. "We'll be able to

clean it up and put a nice bandage on it. Do you think you can walk home, Lizzie, or should Dat carry you?"

"I-i-it-it was a dog," Emma sniffed.

"What was a dog?" Dat asked kindly.

"A dog ran out. A huge black and brown one. He scared Dolly, and she jumped way up and dumped me and Lizzie off."

Dat looked around at the back yards. There was no big dog anywhere, and none of their neighbors seemed to have heard a thing. No doors were open, and no one came running at the sound of the girls' screaming, so Dat guessed it was a stray dog that was just passing through the alley.

They all walked home together, Dat carrying Lizzie, and Mam holding Emma's hand very tightly, while she carried the empty milk jug with the other. Mam and Dat were very thankful the girls were not hurt worse.

Dat went straight to the barn to unhitch Dolly, who was standing inside the big barn door, shaking with fright.

Mam took Lizzie to the bathroom and cleaned the long, deep cut with alcohol on a cotton swab. Then, with a warm washcloth, she carefully cleaned away the dirt and gravel. The alcohol stung, but after the bandage was in place, it felt a lot better. Mam laid her carefully on a clean pillow on the sofa and kissed her cheek. Lizzie felt so much better, although she often wondered where that dog came from and where he was going.

Emma came to sit quietly on the end of the sofa where Lizzie lay. They didn't say a word, just looked at each other with eyes that were filled with concern. You could never be careful enough, driving a pony. And Lizzie was glad Mrs. Zimmerman didn't see her sitting there, yelling as loud as she could.

chapter 11

Playing Cow

It was Thanksgiving Day, and the Glick family was all dressed up. They were going to Uncle James's house for a big Thanksgiving dinner.

It wasn't really cold outside, but they had to wear their shawls and bonnets. Lizzie didn't know why Mam made them wear their shawls. They were so black and scratched the back of her neck terribly. Her bonnet was navy blue and way too big. It felt like she had blinders on, because it was so big she could barely see right or left.

So she walked a little behind everyone else and thought unhappy thoughts. For one thing, she had to wear her purple Sunday dress and Emma had a new one. It was purple, too, almost the exact same shade, but Mam put really pretty buttons on it. Lizzie never had buttons as nice as those, and she wished her bonnet wasn't so big.

She felt ugly, with
an old purple dress.
Then, this morning
Emma said
Lizzie's
cheeks were
not near as
pink as her
own. Lizzie
pulled back
her hand to
smack Emma, but Mam caught it and held it firmly. She
had heard the whole thing, which was good for Emma.

Mornings were like that, though. Especially when
they had to get dressed up and go away. Mam was in
a rush and always telling the girls to hurry up and get
going. It made Lizzie grouchy inside, especially if she
was sleepy. And, the worst thing was Mam doing their
hair. When they went away, Mam always rolled their
hair tighter and more smoothly. She used some kind of
horrible-smelling gel on their hair to make it stay nice
and neat all day. If Lizzie wrinkled her forehead, she felt
that stiff feeling along the side of her head and it made
her uncomfortable. So she always complained, and Mam
always told her the same thing. It would be okay—but
it never was. Then she flopped that huge bonnet on her
head.

So it was really no wonder Lizzie was in a bad mood.
When they came to the gate leading up to the old stone
house, the door burst open and Marvin and Elsie came

flying out. They ran straight up to Emma, grabbed her hands, and said, "Hi, Emma." They found Lizzie and squeezed her hands. "Hi, Lizzie! Boy, are we going to have fun today!"

Emma looked at Marvin and Elsie. "Why?"

Marvin talked enthusiastically about Uncle James's empty cow stable. "We can play cows all day. And you know what else, Emma? Uncle James has that big bull in his pen and he can't get out at all. And he gets mad if you tease him."

Lizzie was thrilled. She forgot all about her stiff hair and big bonnet. This might be lots of fun.

"Come, girls," Mam called. "Dinner's almost ready now, so you have to stay inside till after dinner. Come give me your shawls and bonnets."

They went inside, where a warm, steamy smell enveloped them. Lizzie blinked because the kitchen was darker than outside. She saw Grandma Glick mashing potatoes at the sink, with clouds of steam pouring over her face. She laughed and took off her glasses.

"Well, I can't see my little girls that way," she smiled. Grandpa Glick was seated beside the shining brown coal stove. He reached out and grabbed Lizzie's shawl, pulling her up close to him.

Grandpa Glick was not a warm and cuddly grandfather. He was a minister who preached loud sermons in church, with a voice that boomed. Lizzie often thought he looked like Moses when God gave him the Ten Commandments. He was a bit stern, and when he spoke to Marvin and Elsie, they ran to do his bidding.

But he could also be a big tease, and today Lizzie glanced timidly up into his face. His eyes were twinkling and there was a broad smile on his face.

"Lizzie, do you know why the chicken crossed the road?" All the uncles and Dat laughed when Lizzie said, "I don't know. I guess it wanted to go over to the other side." She said this very seriously, with respect to Grandpa.

"Very good, Lizzie. That's exactly right. That's the real reason the chicken crossed the road. You're not dumb, are you?"

Dat smiled at Lizzie, and Lizzie smiled back. "Come, I'll take off your bonnet." So she went to Dat and he took off her shawl and bonnet. He handed it to Mam, who was walking past with a stack of shawls and bonnets.

Marvin and Elsie stood with Emma, talking excitedly. Lizzie ran over to listen to what they were saying.

Marvin was telling Emma about the tree house he was building. Every day when he had time, he told them, he was building it.

"Come, children, time to sit down and eat now," trilled one of the aunts. Everyone was rushing around, carrying bowls of steaming food. The table was covered with a white tablecloth that had tiny little pink flowers embroidered on the end. The china also had pink and red roses, with crystal clear water glasses set carefully at every plate.

Bowls piled high with creamy mashed potatoes were set along the huge table. Rivers of browned butter ran

across the top. Platters of chicken and stuffing, creamy
yellow corn, and pretty glass dishes of coleslaw filled the
table. There were plates of homemade bread, and deli-
cate little jelly dishes filled with raspberry jelly. Slices of
dark green cucumbers and dark red beets were arranged
in pretty cut glass dishes. There were deviled eggs on
blue egg trays, and applesauce in little glass bowls.

Lizzie, Emma, Marvin, and Elsie slid down a long,
wooden bench. Their plates were a bit smaller than the
grown-ups', and their glasses were not pretty, but plain,
plastic, everyday tumblers. Lizzie wished she was old
enough to eat from the big plates, with fancy glasses to
hold her drink.

They all bowed their heads for a silent grace, or
"patties down." Lizzie wondered if Grandpa Glick fell
asleep, because she couldn't hold her head up for a very
long time, and her nose was terribly itchy. At home,
when her nose was itchy, she always lowered her head
as far as she could. That made it easier to lift one finger
and scratch her nose, so that it was barely noticeable.
But here in the presence of company she couldn't do
that, so she just had an itchy nose, and that was that.

As soon as Grandpa Glick raised his head, the chattering started. It seemed to Lizzie everyone was talking
and nobody was listening. The food was being passed at
an alarming rate, and Lizzie could barely keep up. She
was really hungry, so she piled lots of mashed potatoes
on her plate.

Mam came and stood behind Emma and Lizzie to
help them with the big platter of chicken and stuffing.

She helped Lizzie with the rich, salty gravy and spread butter and raspberry jelly on a slice of homemade bread.

Lizzie ate until she was almost full, but not quite. Some of the aunts teased Emma and Lizzie for heaping their plates so full.

Aunt Sarah tugged on Lizzie's apron, tickling her waist. "No wonder you're getting chubby, Lizzie, the way your plates were piled!"

Lizzie didn't answer, because she was a bit embarassed. She didn't mind being chubby. Besides, Aunt Sarah wasn't skinny, either. So when the chocolate cake and pumpkin pie were passed, Lizzie helped herself to a huge piece of each. That made her feel better, because it tasted so good and comforted her.

As soon as everyone was finished eating, Mam and the aunts passed cups of steaming hot coffee. Marvin looked at Lizzie and sighed. That meant they had to sit there until everyone was finished with their coffee.

Lizzie swung her legs. Emma took a drink from her plastic cup. Elsie scraped her plate with her spoon to clean it well.

Marvin said, low and under his breath, "C'mon. Hurry up and drink your coffee."

"Shhhh!" Elsie warned him.

Lizzie swung her legs some more. Emma asked, "Who is going to be the cow?"

Marvin assured her, "You're all cows. I'm the man."

Elsie glared at him. "You're always the man, Marvin."

"Well, I am a boy!"

"Shh! Patties down," Emma whispered, and everyone

lowered their head. Lizzie didn't say thank you for her food again. She was too excited, thinking of playing cow in a real cow stable.

As soon as Grandpa Glick raised his head, they swung their legs across the wooden bench, and threaded their way through the kitchen full of aunts and babies. They found their sweaters among a heaping pile of shawls and bonnets, and Lizzie was in such a hurry she put her sweater on backward. Elsie really thought that was funny.

They raced out the walk and across the gravel drive, pushing open the big wooden door that led to the cow stable.

Inside, there was a long concrete aisle in the middle covered with white lime. On each side of this wide aisle was a ditch that Marvin called "the drop." On each side of the drop were stalls made of steel pipes, that separated one cow from the other. And each cow had a little bowl that you could press down on a little paddle on the bottom, and water gushed out. Lizzie often wished she'd be allowed to drink out of those little bowls, like a real cow, but Emma said it was too dirty.

Along each side of the cow stable, where the cows' heads were, was another corridor where the feed cart was kept. There were bits of hay scattered around, but never any cow feed or silage, because the cows always licked up every bit of that while they were being milked. But there were no cows in this big, clean barn today, because they were all out in the pasture. They were allowed to play and didn't need to worry about the cows coming in to chase them out.

The most exciting part was the bull's pen in the farthest corner. The bull stayed in there a lot; Lizzie guessed because he was so angry. He stood and watched the children with his head lowered, chewing his cud. He could never break out of those iron bars, so Lizzie was not really afraid, as long as Marvin didn't tease him too much.

They found the express wagon, and Marvin told all the girls to sit in it, because they were cows now, and he was bringing them home from the auction. Elsie bristled at that, because she didn't think they should sit; cows don't sit down! So they all tried to get on their hands and knees on the wagon at one time, but the wagon was too little.

Marvin took off his hat and scratched his head. "Well, Elsie, you stay here, and I'll take just Emma and Lizzie."

"That's dumb, Marvin. Every time we play something, you act like you're the boss. I'm not going to stay here," she pouted.

"Now behave yourself, Elsie. You know you don't all fit in this wagon!" Marvin was quite exasperated.

"I'm not going to," Elsie said, quite firmly.

"Oh, you act just like a cow!" Marvin yelled at Elsie. Lizzie thought that was hilarious. So did Emma. They laughed until they almost fell off the wagon.

"It's not funny," shouted Elsie.

Emma and Lizzie quickly stopped laughing. Elsie looked as if she could burst into tears, and Lizzie pitied her. Marvin was bossy.

Emma said, "Why do we have to be at an auction? Why can't we just walk into a cow pen and then start to play cow?"

"That wouldn't be near as real," Marvin argued. Lizzie was getting tired of this. She didn't know why Marvin thought he had to bring them home from an auction.

"Marvin, just put us in a stall, and let's play once," she said.

Marvin glared at her and threw down the wagon handle. "I'm not going to play cow, then!"

"Well, good!" Elsie chirped, and picked up the wagon handle. "Then I'm the man."

Marvin pushed Elsie away. "No! I'm the man."

"Okay then, if you're the man, we're going to our stalls." And Elsie marched into the stalls, followed by Lizzie and Emma. They dropped down into the clean straw on their hands and knees.

Marvin put his hat squarely on his head and followed them. He took the chain that hung at each stall and fastened it to the neck of their aprons. Lizzie felt like a real cow, and Emma mooed loudly. They collapsed in a fit of giggles, and Elsie gasped, "Emma, cows don't moo that loud!"

Emma only mooed louder, and Marvin told her to stop that; cows do not make near that much noise!

They played all afternoon. When Marvin got too bossy, they unhooked their own snap and went running down the cow stable aisle until he caught them and made them go back. It was wonderful fun. They pressed

down all the paddles on the water bowls until they were
filled to the brim with cold water.

They even tried to taste the cows feed, because Lizzie
said it smelled good. Marvin told her it was because
there was molasses in the feed.

"How do you know?" Elsie asked him, picking a piece
of straw out of her hair. "You don't know if they put
molasses in there or not. I guarantee they don't."

"Oh, yes—they do so! I asked Dat."

"You think you know everything all the time," Elsie
retorted.

Lizzie brushed the lime off her black apron. She
smiled at Emma. Emma smiled back at Lizzie, and they
both knew why they had to smile. They loved Marvin
and Elsie, and they loved to hear them argue, because
Marvin was so fussy. And Elsie was always sure that
Marvin didn't know anything. Of all the people they
knew and loved, Marvin and Elsie were the best.

Their smile faded as they heard a low, rumbling
sound. They all turned and watched, their hearts thud-
ding in their chests, as the low sound echoed again, only
louder.

Marvin grabbed Lizzie's arm. "It's the bull."

Emma's face turned pale. Lizzie chewed her lower lip.
Elsie's eyes were big and round.

Whack! The sound of a dull thud against iron caused
them all to jump in terror.

"Wow!" Marvin breathed.

"He's mad, Marvin!" Lizzie was terrified.

"He can't get out," Marvin announced loudly, but

when Lizzie glanced at him, she saw him swallow. He was afraid, too.

"Let's go in." Elsie sounded as if she was going to cry.

"Let's do," Emma and Lizzie agreed.

But Marvin was fascinated as the angry bull bellowed again. He slammed his forehead into the iron bars and snorted loudly.

A shiver of fear ran up Lizzie's back. Marvin watched the angry creature a while, then said, "Watch!" And he charged toward the bull, yelling at the top of his lungs.

The bull cast a bewildered expression at Marvin, and hopped to the other side of his pen with a stiff-legged gait. He watched warily as Marvin let loose a volley of horrible shouts.

"See?" Marvin laughed. "He's scared."

The girls could see the bull standing away from the bars, and he certainly did not look very angry anymore.

Elsie, Emma, and Lizzie all agreed that Marvin was really a big, brave boy, and he sure knew how to handle a mad bull. They figured he was probably right about cow feed having molasses in it, too.

chapter 12

Emma Is Sick

"Emma! Emma!" Mam's voice brought Lizzie from a deep sleep. It was a cold autumn morning, and the soft, warm flannel sheets were so cozy. Lizzie opened one eye and peeped at Emma. She was still sound asleep and did not answer Mam.

"Emma!"

Mam's voice was a bit louder and more insistent. "Mm-m," Lizzie answered because Emma would still not wake up. She just lay there and went right on sleeping.

"Come, girls," Mam went on. "It's time to get up and get dressed for school."

Lizzie threw back the covers and reached over to shake Emma a bit. She drew back in alarm when she touched Emma's arm. She felt like a heater—her arm was so warm. Lizzie bent over and felt her cheek. It was flushed bright red, and her forehead felt almost hot.

Lizzie shook Emma, saying, "Emma, wake up. Mam called us and it's time to get up."

Emma opened her eyes, blinked, and looked at Lizzie. Her hand flew to her throat. She gasped, coughed, and started crying. She choked, coughed some more, and gave Lizzie a bewildered look.

Lizzie hopped onto her knees and bent over Emma. "Are you alright?"

"N-n-no," Emma cried.

"What's wrong?"

"I don't know. My throat hurts, but I actually hurt all over."

"Do you want me to go tell Mam?" Lizzie was really worried because Emma was not often as sick as this.

"Y-yes." Emma was crying softly.

So Lizzie jumped off the bed and stuck her feet into her soft blue slippers, because the wooden floor was so cold. She slipped through the door and called, "Mam, come here! Emma doesn't feel well!"

Mam was stirring something on the stove, but she turned and asked, "What's wrong with her, Lizzie?"

Lizzie walked over to Mam and peeped into the pan to see what she was stirring. Mam put her arm around Lizzie's soft flannel-clad shoulder and squeezed. "How is my little Lizzie this cold morning?"

Lizzie saw what Mam was stirring. It was hot cocoa, which Lizzie just loved—especially when Mam made fresh shoofly pie. Mam would put a piece of it in a cereal dish and Lizzie poured her mug of hot cocoa over it.

Mam turned off the burner and took Lizzie's hand, "Come, Lizzie, we'll go see what's wrong with Emma."

As they entered the girls' room, Mam became very concerned when she heard Emma's soft crying. She dropped on her knees beside the bed and felt Emma's warm forehead.

"Emma, honey, my goodness—you're warm! Did you feel sick last night when you went to bed?"

"No, not really." Emma sighed. "I just hurt all over and I couldn't sleep for a long time because my legs hurt so much."

"Well, there's no school for you today, that's for sure. You just stay under the warm covers and I'll fix you a nest on the couch," Mam said.

"Can I help you?" Lizzie asked.

Fixing a nest was always something Mam did if they were sick. First she would spread a soft, clean sheet on the living room sofa. Then she put a pretty flowered cover on their pillow, plumped it up comfortably, and let them lie down on the sweet coolness. She allowed them to use soft baby blankets to cover themselves.

And then, best of all, there was a tray. Mam would put orange juice in a small glass, usually a fancy one, and add some buttered toast or milk. Whoever was sick was allowed to have their tray on the sofa, and did not have to eat at the table with the rest of the family. They always felt extra important, having a tray.

While Mam and Lizzie were spreading the sheet, they heard a loud thump from the bedroom. Lizzie ran to see what had happened. Emma lay on a heap beside the dresser, her face completely white. Lizzie screamed and screamed. She was certain Emma had died.

Mam moved swiftly past Lizzie, and with a soft cry of alarm, scooped Emma up in her arms. Quickly, she carried her through the kitchen, bending a bit as she opened the door with one hand. Dat appeared in the kitchen, having heard Lizzie scream.

"What is going on?" He dashed across the kitchen, out to the screened-in porch where Mam was trying to revive Emma with the cold winter air.

"Emma!" she kept repeating over and over, while Dat looked on quite helplessly.

"Let me take her," Dat said.

Mam handed her to Dat, while tears formed in her eyes. Dat talked softly to Emma, asking her to wake up.

Suddenly her body shuddered and her eyes flew open. She started crying as the cold air hit her fever-wracked body.

"Emma, honey, don't cry." Mam reached over and kissed her pale cheek.

"You'll be alright," Dat crooned as he carried her into the warm kitchen. He laid her tenderly on the sofa, while Emma cried softly.

Mam brought her a cold drink of water, but Emma wasn't thirsty and just turned her face away.

"She's really a sick little girl," Dat said.

"Yes, she certainly is. We may as well make an appointment with Dr. Parker as soon as they'll take her." Mam looked worriedly at Emma, then at the clock.

"Lizzie, it's high time for you to get ready for school. My goodness, you'll be late if we don't hurry. Go get your dress on, and I'll comb your hair."

So Lizzie hurried back to the cold bedroom and shivered into her dress. She sat on her unmade bed and pulled on her black stockings. Mam combed her hair, pulling horribly on the snarls, but Lizzie clenched her teeth and didn't say anything.

"There," Mam said, patting her shoulder. "You're all set for school. Lavina will soon be here, so get your coat and bonnet. Lizzie, do you know where your mittens are? You got them wet last night, you know."

"I don't need any," Lizzie said. "It's not really cold this morning." She scooped up her lunchbox, and ran over to the sofa. Bending over Emma, she said softly, "Bye, Emma. I have to go to school now. You have to go to the doctor today. I hope you don't have to get a shot. Bye."

"Bye, Lizzie." Dat was sitting with Emma, waiting for breakfast, and watching her still form. He looked worried.

"Bye, Dat. Bye, Mam," said Lizzie quietly and let

herself out the door and down the stairs.

She waited and waited by the porch post. She watched down the street, hoping to catch sight of Lavina. But there was no Lavina this morning. Instead, a horse and buggy came dashing up the street. Lizzie backed hard against the porch post, because it looked like a really fast horse. The harness had lots of pretty white rings and shiny silver buttons all over it. The buggy did not have a roof on it like Dat's carriage did. It just had a seat out in the open. The young people that weren't married used them. When it rained they had to use a big black umbrella tilted the right way so the rain would stay off them.

Lizzie always thought it would be so much fun to have a ride in an open buggy. But nobody ever asked her to ride in one, and she would never ask anyone, because it would be much too bold.

So she felt her heart pound when the buggy came to a halt, the horse's hooves spraying gravel as the driver called, "Whoa! Whoa there!"

"Are you Lizzie?" The young man tilted back his straw hat and smiled at her. "I'm supposed to take someone to school this morning, because Lavina Lapp is sick. Do you want to go along with me?"

Lizzie took a small step forward, adjusted her bonnet with one hand, clutching her lunchbox more tightly. She looked up at the young man and was overcome with terrible shyness. His hair was long and black, straight as the horse's tail. His eyes were very dark brown and crinkled at the corners when he smiled at her. Lizzie

thought he looked like an Indian she saw in the encyclo-
pedia at school.

She had to clear her throat before she finally managed
to say, "Ye-es, I'm Lizzie. My sister Emma is sick, too."

"C'mon, Lizzie. Give me your hand and I'll help you
up. Here, give me your lunch first. Whoa. Whoa." He
pulled back as the horse lunged forward a bit. "Careful.
Now jump."

A strong hand pulled her small hand up, and—as if by
magic—Lizzie was sitting beside him on the seat. It was
so high! It seemed as if she sat up way too far, and the
horse was too far away from the buggy. It was so deli-
ciously scary!

"C'mon. Gidd-up!" The young man pulled back on
the reins and let loose quickly. Lizzie's head flew back
against the seat as the horse was off to a fast start. The
wind grabbed at her bonnet strings and flapped her
skirt. She reached to tuck it under her legs.

Lizzie looked over at the young man. She couldn't
help but giggle. Her little laugh made him smile, and he
looked down at her.

"Is this your first ride in a buggy?" he asked.

He smiled again when Lizzie's giggles became infec-
tious.

"Yes." Lizzie took a deep breath. "I often wanted to
have a ride, but I don't know anybody that has one."

"You don't know who I am, either, do you?"

"No, but you must know Lavina Lapp, or you
wouldn't be taking me to school."

He smiled down at her. "Smart young lady, aren't

you? Yes, I know her. I work for your Uncle James on the farm three days a week."

"Oh," Lizzie said. She didn't know what else to say, so she just watched the harness flapping up and down on the horse's rump as he trotted at a swift pace.

The air was cold on Lizzie's face, and tears formed in her eyes from the cold wind. She shivered. They were just flying along, she thought. The horse went a lot faster than Red, even if he was smaller.

The young man looked down and asked, "Are you cold? Here, wrap the blanket around you." He handed her a soft, woolen blanket, then reached over and tucked it around her. It was followed by a heavy black canvas blanket that kept all the cold air off Lizzie.

"This big black blanket is called a gum blanket. That's to keep us dry when it rains," he said.

Lizzie didn't know what to say to that, either. She thought about asking him where he kept his big black umbrella, but she didn't really know how to say it right, so she kept quiet.

She was surprised to see the schoolhouse already. The young man pulled on the reins, slowing the horse so they could turn in on the road that went past the school-house. As they pulled up to the school, the children on the porch all stared at Lizzie in amazement. Her little girlfriends put their hands over their mouths and opened their eyes wide. Lizzie felt very important as the young man loosened the gum blanket and helped her off the buggy. He smiled at her as he handed her lunchbox to her.

"There you go, Lizzie. Have a good day at school."

"Thank you," Lizzie remembered to say.

She stepped back as the horse turned to go out the schoolyard gate. All her friends ran up to her as soon as the buggy was gone.

"Lizzie!" squealed Betty. "Who was that? Was it fun? Where's Emma and Lavina?"

Betty was like that. She was Lizzie's favorite friend, although Lizzie had soon learned to love all of them. Betty was the little girl who sat beside her who had on a fancy dress. Sarah was thin and soft-spoken, but very friendly. Lizzie often traded her pretzels for Sarah's popcorn.

So Lizzie pulled herself up tall and said, "He's a hired boy who works for my Uncle James."

"Well, why did he bring you in his buggy?" Betty asked.

"Because Lavina is sick, and I mean it, Betty—my sister Emma is so sick she passed out on the floor. And she has to go to the doctor, and—" Lizzie paused for emphasis. "I guarantee she's going to get a *shot*."

Sarah and Betty gasped. They 'oohed' and 'aahed.' Lizzie went on to tell them how hot Emma's arm had felt and Teacher Sylvia heard her. She smiled to herself. To think this assured young girl was the same one who cried for days in singing class when she first arrived. You could never tell, that was one thing sure.

. . . . .

Lizzie closed her spelling book and put it in her desk. She put her pencils and eraser carefully in her little plastic pencil box. As the pupils took turns to get their hats, bonnets, and coats, Lizzie wondered when the hired boy with his open buggy would come to take her home. She was looking forward to another ride in the buggy.

She went along when her row was called, grabbing her lunchbox from the shelf with one hand, and pulling her bonnet and coat off the hook with the other. She hurried back to her desk, buttoned her coat, and was tying her bonnet securely as they all stood to sing their 'goodbye' song. Everyone rushed out the door when Teacher Sylvia tapped the bell.

"How are you going home, Lizzie?" Betty asked her worriedly.

"Oh, I guess Uncle James's hired boy will soon be here. I'll just wait here on the porch," Lizzie answered.

"Okay. See you tomorrow!" Betty ran backwards, waving as she went. "Bye! See you!"

"Bye!" Lizzie answered. She sat down on the concrete porch and let her legs dangle over the side. She kicked her heels against the hard concrete and watched for a buggy. Everyone was walking home in groups, but it really didn't bother Lizzie—she knew the hired boy would soon be here.

She opened her lunchbox to see if there was anything left to eat. Only her apple, because Lizzie didn't really like apples. Especially not the sour ones, and this one looked like the kind that would pucker her mouth horribly. So she closed her lunchbox, kicked her heels again, and wriggled around a bit on the hard concrete so she would be more comfortable.

Inside the schoolhouse, Teacher Sylvia tackled an
unusually large amount of workbooks to be corrected.
It had really been a trying day, and she sent a prayer
heavenward for strength and patience to cope with other
days such as this one. She had no idea little Lizzie Glick
sat on the porch, patiently waiting for her ride.

Lizzie was thoroughly tired of waiting. She wondered
if it would be alright if she started walking. She knew
which side of the road they usually walked on, and if she
was very careful, she could walk home.

Resolutely, she jumped off the porch and started off.
Out past the gate, swinging her lunchbox, Lizzie walked
down the road at a fast pace. She was only a small black
figure, with her bright blue bonnet , and her yellow
lunchbox bobbing with every step. She chewed her lip
and glanced nervously up and down the road when she
reached the crossroad. Turning
left, she walked carefully on the
gravel beside the road, looking
neither left nor right.

Cars whizzed past, but she
kept marching on. She guessed
if everyone forgot about her,
she'd just have to take care of
herself. Emma would be so
amazed that she walked home
all alone. And she bet Dat would
let her drive the pony all by
herself if she walked
home from school by

herself. Actually, she felt quite grownup, so she straightened her back and walked along as tall as she could. The
gravel crunched under her feet, and leaves whirled out
of the woods beside her. It was getting a bit windy, but
Lizzie thought the wind would push her along, because
it was blowing against her back.

When she reached the small town where they lived,
a tractor and wagon came putt-putting down the road.
Lizzie quickly jumped up on the sidewalk and stopped.
She glared at the driver because she thought he was
not watching one tiny bit where he was going. He was
almost driving on her strip of gravel, and he should be
more careful.

After that, she marched on down the sidewalk until she was almost at their house. She was glad to see
Dat's harness shop sign swinging high up in front of the
porch. She waited until two cars passed, then she burst
into a fast run, dashing quickly across the road.

Up the stairs, banging the screen door on the porch,
she opened the door and yelled loudly, "Mam!"

Mam came hurrying into the kitchen. "Shhh! Shh,
Lizzie. Emma is finally sleeping. Be quiet." She held her
finger to Lizzie's mouth, and hugged her with her other
arm. "How did you get home, Lizzie?"

"I walked."

"You what?" Mam was incredulous.

"I walked home."

"Not all by yourself, Lizzie! Please don't tell me you
walked home all by yourself!"

"Yes, I did, Mam."

"Why, Lizzie? Why did you do it? Someone could have picked you up!"

Lizzie looked into Mam's face, because suddenly she sounded like this was terrible. Mam actually looked very, very frightened.

"Well, the hired boy who took me to school didn't come to get me, and I was really tired of waiting, so I walked."

"Where in the world was Teacher Sylvia?" asked Mam.

"Inside, I guess," Lizzie responded.

"Ach, my!" Mam plopped onto a chair and covered her face with her hands. "First Emma gets rheumatic fever and then you walk home from school alone. I don't know if I want to cry or scream!" Mam exclaimed.

"I made it, Mam. Don't worry." Lizzie reached up her chubby little hand and patted Mam's cheek. "Don't worry, Mam."

Tears of relief, mixed with worry, ran down Mam's face as she gathered Lizzie into her arms. Lizzie felt so secure, so warm and safe, in the circle of her mother's arms.

"What is wrong with Emma, Mam?" Lizzie searched her mother's face, as Mam wiped her eyes with a white handkerchief. She lifted her glasses and wiped her cheeks.

"Well, Lizzie, it looks as if you'll have to go to school alone for a long time. She has rheumatic fever, which means she is a very sick little girl. She has to stay in bed for many weeks so her heart doesn't get damaged by the disease. So you will have to help her at home with her schoolwork, and go to school with Lavina Lapp all by yourself."

"You mean she can't even get out of bed? Not even to eat and go to the bathroom?" Lizzie couldn't believe what her mother was saying.

"No, she can walk around a little, but it's mostly bed rest for her," Mam said.

Lizzie sat down on a chair, let her shoulders slump, and felt so lonely and so much like crying. She just sat there for a long time with her coat and bonnet on, staring at the floor and feeling very, very sad. And because Mam just sat there with her, saying nothing, Lizzie guessed she must be sad, too.

The Christmas Program

It was Christmas. Or almost Christmas. Lizzie was studying every day to say her poem for the Christmas program at school. The weather turned colder, snow was in the air, and every day Lizzie asked her mother how long till Christmas.

Emma still had to stay in bed or on the couch. Her face was pale, and she coughed a lot. Every day she had to take gross-looking medicine. Mam had to take her to the doctor every week, and when they came home, Emma was often so tired, she slept all afternoon.

Lizzie felt terribly sorry for Emma. She did all the kind things she could think of—at first, anyway. She brought her a tissue, or a cold drink, or even let her have her best tablet and pen for one whole day. They never fought, because Lizzie pitied Emma, having to stay in bed like that.

But today Lizzie was tired of everything. It was cold—too cold to play outside with Mandy, because Mandy was too little. It was Saturday, so she couldn't go to school. Emma lay on the couch and looked more bored and gloomy than usual.

Lizzie thought of her poem that she still did not know quite perfectly. "Emma, help me with my Christmas poem."

"No."

"Emma, please? I don't know it very well," Lizzie said.

"It makes me tired, listening to you say that dumb poem over and over and over," Emma rolled on her side, pulled up her blanket, and looked at the back of the couch.

Suddenly a hot anger welled up in Lizzie. She slid off the chair, walked over to Emma, and slapped her hard on her head.

"Ow! Ow! Ouch! Oh!" Emma yelled and cried in a loud voice, and all this was followed by a fit of severe coughing.

Lizzie was filled with fear and terrible remorse. What had she done? Oh, this was truly the most terrible thing she had done to Emma. Amid Emma's howls and coughs, Lizzie looked wildly to the kitchen and to the top of the stairs that went down to Dat's harness shop. She knew, with a dreadful certainty, that she had definitely gotten herself into some big trouble.

She looked at the top of the stairs again, and ran blindly into her room. The only sensible thought was to try to hide somewhere. But where?

She tried wriggling under her bed, but it was so tight, and there was so much dust, that she wriggled back out again. She could faintly hear Emma's coughs and her crying. She stood still and listened, her hands clasped against the pounding of her heart. Sure enough, just as she had feared, she heard the steady steps of her father coming up the stairs.

Looking desperately around her bedroom, Lizzie thought of the closet. Quickly, she yanked open the door and threw herself down in the darkest corner. She winced as the sharp heel of a shoe dug into her stomach. She grabbed the shoe and threw it into the other corner, but she still felt something jabbing at her leg. She pushed a toy away and sat up, circling her knees with her arms to make herself as tiny as possible.

Now there was nothing to do but sit there as quietly as she could, hoping Emma would quit her loud crying and coughing before Dat heard her. Emma was acting like such a baby since she was sick anyway. Everybody had to be nice, everybody pitied her, and Lizzie was just getting so tired of it.

She heard Dat's low voice, then Mam's higher tone. Emma was still coughing, and Lizzie thought she was doing all that on purpose. Soon she heard Dat calling her name. It was not a pleasant call. It was loud and severe, as if he was not one bit happy about Lizzie slapping Emma.

Lizzie scooted back a bit farther, her heart beating loudly. It seemed as if Dat could hear her heart, even though she never said one word.

Dat called again. He was coming closer. Lizzie knew
she should get off the closet floor and let Dat know
where she was. She just couldn't, because she knew now
without a doubt that she was going to be disciplined.
Dat was definitely not happy.

She wondered if it would help if she came out of the
dark closet and told Dat she was sorry. But maybe, just
maybe, if she stayed in there, nobody would find her
that whole day and maybe into the night. Then they
would think someone kidnapped her or she died and
they'd all be so glad to see her again, she would never
get disciplined again as long as she lived. They would always love her extra much, even if Emma had rheumatic
fever. And if Emma screamed and cried they would tell
her to be quiet.

Her thoughts were brought to a halt quite rudely by
the closet door being yanked open.

"Lizzie!" Dat peered into the dark recesses of the
closet. "Are you in there, Lizzie?"

"N-n-no," Lizzie quavered.

Dat straightened up and looked away. Lizzie searched
his face, and for one moment she thought Dat looked as
if he was getting ready to laugh. But he certainly was
not laughing when he reached down and pulled Lizzie
out of the closet.

"Lizzie," he said sternly, "why did you smack Emma
like that?"

"I-I don't know." Lizzie said miserably.

"Lizzie." Dat was very serious. "You know you girls are not allowed to smack each other at any time, and especially not if Emma doesn't feel well."

Lizzie started crying, mostly because she was so sure Dat would not find her, but he did. And why did she always end up getting in trouble when Emma didn't?

Dat sat down on Lizzie's bed and held her till she stopped crying. "Lizzie, now listen. Emma is sick and that means she doesn't feel well, so she gets tired easily. She really didn't want to listen to your poem because she doesn't feel half as good as you do."

Lizzie sniffed. She marched over to the dresser and yanked a tissue out of the box. She blew her nose and wiped it carefully.

"Dat, it's always my fault. Why am I always the one to be disciplined, and not Emma?" Lizzie asked.

"Not always, Lizzie."

"Oh, yes. She called my poem stupid," Lizzie said. "She should be disciplined for that, Dat."

Dat sighed. He looked at Lizzie. He thought she did not look very humbled or sorry. She just stood there and looked at him with her straightforward gaze, and he almost flinched under it. Dat sighed again. There was surely a huge difference in Lizzie and Emma, no doubt.

"Well, Lizzie, we can't spank Emma for that. Not when she's sick. Your poem is not stupid; she was just tired, that's all. Now you must promise me you will never hit Emma on the head again," Dat said.

Lizzie bit her lip, and turned back to the tissue box. "I promise," she said quietly.

But Dat had an uneasy feeling that her promise was not very sincere.

.   .   .   .   .

The snow came down in great white flakes, settling on all the housetops and on every tree. Little puffs of snow flew out from under Red's feet as he trotted down the road to Lizzie's school.

Inside the schoolhouse all the children were excited. The white sheets were hung across a wire that was stretched along the front of the room. The blackboard was decorated with a manger scene, all done with bright-colored chalk. It was truly the most beautiful thing Lizzie had ever seen, and she could not wait until Dat and Mam came to school today to see it.

There were paper candy canes with different-colored ribbons on the windows. Every wall was decorated with Christmas art. Poinsettias in colorful foil-covered pots stood on Teacher Sylvia's desk. Paper snowflakes dangled from strings taped to the ceiling, and when the door opened, they all danced merrily.

Today was the Christmas program at Lizzie's school. Everyone wore their prettiest red or green dress, and their Sunday shoes if their sneakers were too worn out. Lizzie wore her Sunday shoes, because Mam said she was allowed to. She felt very dressed up, and tried hard not to spill any juice from her lunchbox on her black Sunday apron.

She stood by the window and watched the pretty snowflakes coming down from the sky. Every horse and buggy that came through the gate was not her Dat and Red. So she watched the snowflakes, occasionally peering down the road for their horse.

There they came! Lizzie's heart swelled with excitement. This one was Red! He trotted swiftly, his head held high, and when Dat pulled up to the schoolhouse, he pranced on his feet, because he wanted to run some more.

Lizzie went to the door when Mam came in, carrying Mandy. "Hi, Mandy! Come, Mandy. Mam, give her to me. Come, Mandy."

Lizzie was fairly dancing around them both, until Mam laughed and looked at some of the other mothers. "Nothing quite like a Christmas program to get the children excited, is there?" she asked Betty's mother, who laughingly agreed. While the mothers found their seats, Lizzie took Mandy's hand and showed her all the pretty things on the walls.

The schoolroom slowly filled up as all the parents found a seat. Some English people that Lizzie did not know came in, too, and Teacher Sylvia found a seat for

them. Lizzie guessed she must know them, because she
was talking to them and smiling a lot.

After Teacher Sylvia had helped everyone be seated,
she tapped a bell lightly, and everyone quieted down
instantly. She told all the pupils to go behind the curtain
and to be really quiet, please.

Lizzie really hated being behind that curtain. The
big girls were so bossy, and there was no place to sit,
so Lizzie had to stand until she was so tired of it she
thought she'd faint. And if you pushed or shoved someone away so you could sit for a little while, you often got
a grouchy look or sometimes you even got pinched.

All the pupils had done this quite often, practicing
for the program. Everyone knew their parts well, Lizzie
thought. She knew her poem perfectly, and half of the
other children's, as well. Lizzie guessed she must be
pretty smart, because she could say almost everyone's
poem. And once, when she was reciting them to Mandy,
she saw Mam raise her eyebrows to Dat, and Dat smiled
and shook his head. Lizzie bet they had a fit how much
she could say.

After Lizzie's spanking, Emma felt bad and listened
to her saying her poem over and over, until Lizzie knew
it very thoroughly. *Emma is nice,* Lizzie thought after
that—*actually nicer than I am.*

The pupils opened the program with a rousing rendition of a welcome song, to the tune of "Reuben and Rachel." Lizzie loved to sing that song, and even if she was
small and stood in the front row, she sang as loudly as

she could. They also sang "Joy to the World" and other songs, before all filing back in perfect order to stand in their allotted space behind the curtain again.

Betty whispered very quietly to Lizzie. Lizzie didn't understand her at first, so she said, "What?"

As quickly as possible, Lizzie felt a hard pinch on her upper arm. She looked up in embarassment, to find Lavina Lapp holding her forefinger to her mouth in a gesture meaning "Shhh!" Her eyebrows were drawn down really far, so Lizzie knew this was serious today, at the real Christmas program. She had better be really quiet.

One by one the children took turns reciting their poems. They all filed out to sing three more songs. One song was "Jingle Bells," which was Lizzie's favorite. She almost always had to giggle when they sang the chorus, and today was no exception. So she looked steadily at one snowflake and thought sad thoughts for a little while so she would not giggle.

After they all filed back behind the curtain, Lizzie knew it was her turn to say her poem. She was excited and wanted to say it nice and clear, because she knew she could.

She had a long poem for a little girl, but she was quite confident in her own ability. Her heart beat faster, but she stood straight and tall. She put her hands behind her back and started speaking loud and clear.

Suddenly, to her horror, she heard Teacher Sylvia say, "No, no," and in the same moment she saw Mam shake her head back and forth.

She grew warm all over, and quickly raised her hand to her mouth. She was saying one of the upper grade boys' poems!

Her eyes blinked rapidly as her mind adjusted to her own poem. She smiled a sheepish little smile, and started over. Some of the parents laughed, and a few looked like they felt sorry for Lizzie.

After she remembered her own poem, she recited it loud and clear, verse after verse. She didn't stumble once. She felt very proud of herself for saying it, because it really was a long one.

After the "goodbye" song, Teacher Sylvia tapped her bell again and the program was over. The children tumbled out of the curtains while the parents clapped their hands in appreciation.

Lizzie was glad to find Dat and Mam. Dat smiled affectionately at Lizzie and said, "That's what happens when you learn half of the school's poems instead of sticking to your own."

Lizzie supposed that was true, but she still never stopped saying the other children's poems at Christmas.

chapter 14

A Visit from Doddy Millers

Mam had an extra sparkle in her eyes this morning, Lizzie could tell. She had opened a letter yesterday from her parents who lived in Ohio. She had exclaimed at one point, "Oh, good!" and went on reading the letter.

"What?" Emma had asked from her perch on the couch.

"Oh, Doddy Millers are coming in four days! I can hardly believe they'll be staying for almost a week!"

Mam was so happy after that, she even cooked Dat's favorite supper that evening—rivel soup. Lizzie just did not like rivel soup, because of the rivels, but Dat just loved it. Lizzie had watched Mam make rivels, with flour and eggs. It looked like a sticky mess, and when she put the whole batch in milk and added brown butter, Lizzie always thought it looked like lumps of paste she used at school.

Now this morning, Mam set a steaming bowl of oatmeal on the table. Turning, she got the dish of brown sugar and plopped it down. She was singing and her movements were faster than usual.

"There you go, Lizzie. Now eat or you'll be late for school," she said.

"Why can't I stay at home today? I could help you clean up and get ready for Doddy Millers." Lizzie poked her finger in her dish of oatmeal. She withdrew it again just as fast.

"Ouch—that's hot!" she grimaced.

"Well, don't stick your hand in there. It is hot. Here, let me put sugar on it."

"I hate oatmeal," Lizzie pouted.

"Why?" asked Mam.

"It's bumpy, like rivel soup—that's why," said Lizzie.

"Lizzie, you should be thankful for oatmeal. You know what Mommy Miller used to make for all of us

at home? Before I married Dat, there were ten of us children and she cooked cornmeal and we ate that with sugar and milk on it, just like oatmeal."

"Ewww." Lizzie wrinkled her nose. She tasted her oatmeal. It wasn't sweet enough, so she added more brown sugar, tasted it again, and added another spoonful. Her oatmeal was turning darker in color, and when she tasted it again, it was too sweet. She could hardly eat it. She wished she hadn't put so much sugar in it.

"This isn't good, Mam," Lizzie announced.

Mam came over and looked at her oatmeal. She tasted it, swallowed, and looked sternly at Lizzie.

"How much sugar did you put in there?"

"Not much," said Lizzie.

"Well, I guess you'll have to go to school without breakfast. Why are you being so difficult this morning?" Mam asked.

"My stomach hurts." Lizzie drew her eyebrows in and rubbed her stomach.

"I doubt it, Lizzie. You just have the Doddy Miller fever, and want to stay here, afraid you'll miss something. They're not coming for four days yet, so you'll have plenty of time to help me get ready."

"Are they coming on the train?" Lizzie asked.

"Yes, Lizzie. Now get your coat. It's time for Lavina to come." Mam was very firm.

So Lizzie trudged off to school, wishing she could stay at home. It would be much more exciting to help get the house clean and bake good things than to go to school for four more days.

That whole day hardly anything went well. Sarah
wouldn't trade her popcorn, and Betty didn't want to
play Freeze Tag at recess. Plus, she was wearing another
new dress that had lots of lines going straight across
the fabric, and Lizzie thought it was really pretty. She
wished her dress looked so new and fancy, and every
time she looked at her own navy blue dress, she felt
unhappy.

Then, at recess, she fell across a base, and her dress
flew up above her knees. She was so humiliated and so
terribly unhappy about everything, she went into the
bathroom with her chin held high. After she was inside,
she put the little hook through the ring to lock the door,
sat down, and cried huge tears. After she wiped her eyes
and came back out to the Freeze Tag game, Betty looked
at her closely.

"What's wrong," she inquired bluntly.

"Nothing," Lizzie sniffed.

"Were you crying?" she asked.

"No!" yelled Lizzie. "Go away!"

"Boy, you're grouchy, Lizzie." Betty looked hurt.

"I am not! Go away!"

So Betty went to play with Sarah, and Lizzie felt
worse than ever.

On the way home that evening, Lavina Lapp told her
she was fatter than Betty or Sarah. "You must like to
eat, don't you?" she smiled.

Lizzie didn't answer because she didn't know what to
say. All she wanted to do was go home and lay her head
on Mam's shoulder and cry.

When she walked into the kitchen calling for Mam, there was a strange quietness. She couldn't hear Mandy or Mam, and Emma was sound asleep on the couch.

Suddenly the bathroom door opened and a young girl walked out. "Oh, you must be Lizzie. I'm Rachel. Come here and I'll tell you a happy surprise," she said.

Lizzie liked her already. She had a really pretty smile, and she was so friendly and happy. Her hair was jet black and she had brown eyes that twinkled at Lizzie in the most delightful way. So Lizzie put her lunchbox carefully on the counter and walked shyly over to Rachel.

Rachel leaned forward and said, "You guess what!"

"What?" Lizzie had to smile, because Rachel was beaming so excitedly.

Rachel took Lizzie by the arms and squeezed gently. "Your Mam and Dat are at the hospital. And you have a tiny little baby brother. A boy!"

"What?" Lizzie just could not think of one thing to say. "A real one?"

Rachel laughed a lovely, husky laugh that Lizzie loved to listen to. She didn't know what was the happiest thing to think about—a new baby brother or Rachel's laugh.

So Lizzie just sat down and sighed. She clasped her hands on her lap and watched Rachel and sighed again. "Is he tiny?" she giggled.

"I don't know, Lizzie. I haven't seen him yet. Your Dat will soon be home, then he can tell us more about him," she said, tucking the covers over Emma's shoulder.

"What is his name? Is he cute?" Lizzie kept thinking questions about this new baby brother. "Do you think Mam will let me hold him or not? And what about Doddy Millers coming? Who will go to the train station to meet them? Do you think our baby brother will cry a lot?"

"Oh my, Lizzie." Rachel's husky laugh rang out again. "You really are a question box, aren't you?"

Lizzie smiled up at Rachel, and was rewarded with a good sound hug. It was almost as good as eating shoofly pie and cocoa. Lizzie fell soundly in love with their new "maud" named Rachel.

.   .   .   .   .   .

Lizzie fluffed up a pillow on the couch. She told Mandy to put away her toys, watching nervously as every car passed on the road below. Today Dat was bringing Mam and their new baby brother home, and tomorrow was the day Doddy Millers were arriving. Lizzie was in a state of feverish excitement.

Suddenly the kitchen door opened slowly, and there stood Mam! She looked so strange and so pale, that Lizzie felt shy. Mandy made a dash across the kitchen straight into Mam's arms. Emma smiled shyly and said, "Hello, Mam," from her pillow on the couch.

Lizzie was rooted to her chair, feeling so strange, because she didn't know whether to laugh or cry. So she just sat there and chewed on her lower lip.

Dat followed close behind Mam carrying a little blue bundle. His face was wreathed in smiles. Carefully he set down the diaper bag he was carrying and bent over the couch to Emma.

"Emma, look at your brother. His name is Jason, and he looks a lot like Lizzie."

Emma whispered, "Jason?" She lifted the blue blanket and exclaimed softly, "Aww, he's cute! Can I hold him, Dat?"

Dat smiled and lowered the little blue bundle into Emma's lap while Emma stroked the little cheeks and touched his downy hair.

Lizzie slowly got up from her chair and carefully walked over to the couch. She peered under the flap of the soft, woolly blanket. She took a good long look at her new baby brother, and was suddenly overcome with horror. He was so ugly and so bright red, she could not imagine ever letting Mam take him to church. His eyes were closed, but there were so many deep wrinkles around his eyes. Lizzie could not imagine how he could ever see around all that skin. His nose was big and puffy and his mouth was much too big for his face.

She felt Mam come up behind her and put her arm around her shoulders. Lizzie leaned against Mam and tried hard to feel normal and smile — at least smile enough to be nice. But she wished so much her new baby brother wasn't so ugly.

"Isn't he sweet, Lizzie? You may hold him, too. Emma, may Lizzie hold Baby Jason now?" Mam asked.

"I–I don't want to hold him. Emma may." And much to her shame, Lizzie started to cry. Mandy dashed over, and peered anxiously into Lizzie's face.

"Don't cry, Lizzie." She put her arm protectively around Lizzie.

"What's wrong? Come, Lizzie." Mam sat down on a soft chair and just held Lizzie till she finished crying. "Now tell me what's wrong."

But Lizzie never really did tell Mam the real reason she cried. She just told her that her head hurt, because it wasn't nice to say Jason was ugly. But he really was.

.   .   .   .   .

The next day Doddy Millers arrived. Dat hired a driver to go to the big city where the train station was located. Lizzie had to go to school, so she was not allowed to go along.

When she came home from school, she saw Doddy Miller as soon as she came into the kitchen. He was sitting at the table, eating a slice of shoofly pie and drinking coffee.

His hair and beard were snow white, and his eyes were very light blue. He had a long, crooked nose that had lots of red and purple veins on it. He wore a blue denim shirt and darker blue denim pants.

"Here she comes! Here comes my Lizzie!" He reached out and caught Lizzie, enveloping her in a bear hug.

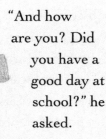

"And how are you? Did you have a good day at school?" he asked.

"Yes! I had a good day, Doddy. Did you like your train ride? Did it go fast?" Lizzie asked.

"Oh my, yes, Lizzie. That train goes a-flying," said Doddy.

Lizzie settled herself at his knee, anticipating a long conversation with Doddy Miller. He was one of Lizzie's favorite people.

Mommy Miller joined them at the table, reaching out to take Lizzie's hand. "Hello, Lizzie!" she said in her quiet voice. She was small featured, and her hair was snowy white, too. She had a soft, round stomach, and narrow shoulders. Because they lived in Ohio, their "ordnung," or church rules, were different, so Mommy's dress and covering were made differently than Mam's or Lizzie's.

Mommy Miller was soft-spoken and never had as much to say as Doddy. But today she was talkative, and Lizzie thought she was excited about Baby Jason, probably.

Mam sat on the couch with Emma, and beamed with pleasure. Everybody was so happy, and Lizzie was so glad to see her grandparents, she did a fancy little whirl on her way to the sink with Doddy's empty shoofly dish. Mandy tried it, too, but fell flat on her back. Everyone laughed as she got up and tried again.

Emma was holding Baby Jason again. Lizzie peeped at him, considering his facial features quietly. Really, there might be a tiny bit of improvement. Lizzie was so relieved to notice that he wasn't quite as bright red as the first time she saw him. She still didn't like to hold him though—she just liked to sit beside Emma when she held him. It made Lizzie nervous to hold a baby. They were too soft and slippery, and Mam said you had to hold their head carefully. Lizzie was always afraid she had the wrong end up.

Doddy Miller was watching Lizzie carefully look at the new baby brother. A smile tugged at the corner of his mouth, because he could see Lizzie's thoughts, the way her eyes looked concerned.

"Don't you think he's cute, Lizzie?" he asked.

"Well . . ." Lizzie hesitated.

"Now, c'mon—he looks a lot like you," Doddy said.

"No, he doesn't, Doddy. You know he doesn't!" she burst out.

Doddy laughed a good, hearty laugh and slapped his knee.

Mommy Miller said, "Now, Abe."

But Lizzie caught the twinkle in Doddy's eye, and she couldn't help but laugh with him. She knew, she just knew for certain, that Doddy didn't think Baby Jason was very cute. She loved Doddy Miller truly with all her heart, because with him she did not have to pretend Baby Jason was cute. She knew he didn't think so, either.

chapter 15

Rachel

While Doddy Millers stayed at
the Glicks, the days were filled
with happy moments. Mommy showed Emma
how to embroider, and even gave her a little wooden
ring called a hoop, that you pinched the fabric into.

On this fabric was a light blue outline of a bird and
a birdhouse. Mommy helped Emma thread her needle
with three strands of embroidery thread, and showed
her how to take tiny little stitches that looked as if she
was sewing backward, but she really wasn't. Emma sat
for hours, contentedly trying to do neat, tiny stitches like
Mommy did.

Mommy gave Lizzie a little square metal frame that
had prongs sticking up, which looked like teeth. Along
with this red frame there was a plastic bag filled with
loops of stretchable fabric. There was also a blue hook.
That was to catch one end of a stretchable loop and

hook it on one of the metal teeth on the frame. After you did a whole row of these loops, you went across the other way, weaving the loops up and down, up and down, through the loops that were already attached. After they were all woven through, it was a potholder for Mam to use when she got a cake out of the oven.

It was hard to get it right, and Lizzie chewed her lip, bit her tongue, and got a very stiff neck if she sat there too long. Doddy Miller helped her intertwine the ends of the loops together to finish it.

Mommy cooked cornmeal mush and they ate it with sugar and milk. Actually, Lizzie thought it tasted a lot like the cow feed in Uncle James's stable. But when Mommy asked Lizzie if she liked it, she smiled and nodded her head politely. She figured if Doddy Miller could eat it, she could, too.

But too soon the day came when they had to leave. Lizzie felt sad; she always did when it was time for Doddys to leave. But Mam smiled bravely as she said her goodbyes, so Lizzie and Emma were brave, too. Dat looked at Mam so lovingly, that Lizzie thought as nice as Dat was, it must be alright for Mam.

And then Rachel came.

After Doddy Millers took the train home to Ohio, Rachel came back to Lizzie's house. She was wearing a royal blue dress with a black apron, which made her hair shine almost blue-black. They were smoothed back to a satiny sheen. Her dark brown eyes twinkled at Lizzie as she set her small overnight suitcase on the table.

Mam said, "Oh, there you are, Rachel." She laughed as she sat down tiredly. "I'm almost embarrassed to tell you how much laundry there is, and what a mess this house is in! But I am so very glad you're here."

"Oh my, don't you worry. I'm sure I've done more laundry than yours," Rachel laughed. She was already rolling up her sleeves. "If you'll tell me where to put my suitcase, I'll put it away and get started right away. Or did you want me to wash the breakfast dishes first?"

"Well, since this is Saturday and Lizzie is home from school, maybe she can help me do the dishes and you can start the laundry. Would that be okay, Rachel?" Mam asked.

"Sure," she smiled.

"You can put your suitcase in the girls' room. Are you planning on staying until tomorrow, or why did you bring one?" asked Mam.

"Oh, I . . ." Rachel's long lashes swept her cheeks, and she blushed as she said, "If it's alright, I'll get ready here and have—I mean, I'll get picked up here tonight."

"Why, of course! You can get ready here! And who, may I ask, is picking you up?"

Rachel was still blushing, but she giggled and said, "You'll have to wait and see!"

She disappeared into the girls' bedroom, but soon returned carrying some nighties and dresses that had been strewn across the floor. "I'll just wash whatever I find, if that's alright," she said.

"Yes, of course," Mam replied.

So Rachel set to work, whistling as she carried the hampers down the stairs to the kettle house.

Almost every Amish family had a kettle house. It wasn't really a house with a kettle in it, but it was where the washing was done. Because there was no electricity, the wringer washer was run by a small gas engine attached to the washing machine. Years ago, they had a huge iron kettle built into a brick oven where fire was built under the kettle to heat the wash water. That was why Amish people called their laundry rooms "the kettle house."

That was also the room Lizzie and Emma kept their boots and outdoor clothes. Dat kept his hat and coat on hooks on the wall, and there was a sink with soap and a towel where he washed his hands. Because Dat worked in a harness shop, he had to use a special hand cleaner to wash the oily black harness odor from his hands.

It was always warm in the kettle house because a coal stove called "Bucket-A-Day" heated the water in the hot water heater.

Sometimes Emma and Lizzie had to clean the kettle house on Saturday. But today Lizzie guessed Rachel would do it, since she was down there doing all that washing, anyway.

Lizzie sighed. Mam looked at her and said, "Well, buzy Lizzie! Looks like you'll be my helper to get these dishes done." Mam looked pale and tired. Lizzie guessed she was not sleeping very well, having to feed Jason so often. She pitied Mam, because Jason wasn't very cute, and he cried a lot. Lizzie thought he would be better-looking if he wasn't so grouchy all the time. Mam said he had colic, but just a touch of it.

Because Lizzie pitied Mam, she didn't complain as she pulled a small stepstool over to the sink. She fit the plug tightly in the bottom, squirted lots of liquid dish detergent, and ran the hot water. First, she took both hands and swished them back and forth as hard as she could to make lots of suds. Then she started scrubbing a plate.

Mam came over to look over her shoulder. "Lizzie, not so much dish soap. And wash the glasses first, not the plates. Remember—first the glasses, then the plates and serving dishes, and last, the pots and pans."

"Oh," said Lizzie. She couldn't see any sense in that. What did it matter in which order you washed dishes? They were all dishes, and they were all dirty. But she didn't say so, because another reason she felt sorry for Mam was because Doddy Millers had just gone back home to Ohio.

So she washed the glasses and looked over the stack of unwashed dishes. There were so many, it looked absolutely hopeless. She looked at the huge pile of suds and wondered if the soap suds would stick to her chin. She lowered her head and stuck her chin into the suds, patting some of them on her face to form a beard. They stuck! Lizzie giggled and put some on her eyebrows.

"Hey!"

Lizzie jumped with surprise. She turned around very quickly and was embarrassed to see Rachel standing behind her.

"What are you doing, little dishwasher?" Rachel

laughed her husky laugh as she caught sight of Lizzie's soapsuds on her face.

Lizzie laughed with her.

"Oh, I wondered if these soapsuds would stick to my face, and they do," Lizzie said.

"Here—I'll wash and you may dry. The white clothes are washing for a while, so I'll help you with the dishes," Rachel said. With that, she handed Lizzie a tea towel and plunged her hands into the mountain of suds.

"Why do you have so much soap?"

"Because in pictures, English people use so much. Their soap bubbles way up out of the sink. Amish people don't use enough soap," Lizzie said, quite seriously.

Rachel threw back her head and laughed. "Oh, Lizzie, you are quite a Lizzie. How do you know how many soapsuds English people use?" she asked.

"They just do," Lizzie answered.

Lizzie was amazed how fast Rachel washed the dishes. Around and around went the sponge, on plates, bowls, and cups. Pots and pans were grasped very firmly by the handle, while she whirled the sponge around the inside. As she worked, she sang, "How I long for the days when I shall meet her; If it be where the angels sweetly sing."

Lizzie watched Rachel in awe. She was so pretty, and when she sang it sounded so sweet—almost like a bird. Lizzie wanted to be grown-up and look exactly like Rachel. But she couldn't, because she didn't have shiny black hair or brown eyes. She could practice singing like Rachel. She wondered if Rachel had a boyfriend, but she was much too shy to ask.

Rachel finished the dishes, and started wiping the counter. She moved everything and wiped under it, even the canister set. She scrubbed the stove top, wringing out the dishrag with her strong arms, wiping it till it shone like glass. Lizzie was convinced Rachel was absolutely wonderful.

After the dishes were finished, Rachel went to do the washing. Lizzie wandered into the living room to find Emma, who was reading quietly. Lizzie bounced onto the couch and Emma's book flew out of her hands. She looked at Lizzie.

"Lizzie, watch it! Can't you sit down nicely?"

"Emma, when are you ever going to get better. It's not fun if you can't play with me anymore." Lizzie lay back against the couch and kicked her legs hard.

"I know," Emma said.

"Well, are you getting better? Did the doctor say you are?" asked Lizzie.

"Oh, yes, of course I am," Emma said.

"How do you know?" Lizzie asked.

"Because."

"Did he say?"

"Did who say?"

"The doctor."

Emma smoothed her hair back. There were stains on her nightgown, and her teeth needed to be brushed. Her faced looked so pale and her hair looked scraggly. Lizzie suddenly felt sorry for Emma. It would not be fun to have rheumatic fever.

"Lizzie, you know that dark brown stuff I have to

drink in the morning? That Oza Compound?" Emma asked.

"Yes?" Lizzie raised one eyebrow and stuck out her tongue, clutching her stomach. "That stuff."

"Well, it is horrible to drink, but Dat says he thinks that is really helping me get better."

"Goody." And Lizzie meant it with all her heart. She so wanted Emma to be healthy again.

"Do you want to play Chutes and Ladders, Emma?" Lizzie asked kindly.

"Do you?" Emma asked.

"If you do."

"Okay, we'll play," Emma said.

Lizzie ran to get the game, and plopped it on the card table beside Emma's bed. They played for a long time, giggling and laughing over who got to climb ladders and who had to fall down the chutes.

Their play was interrupted by a loud wail from the bedroom. Mam had gone to take a nap, because Baby Jason had not slept well during the night. But now he was awake and screaming as loud as he could.

Lizzie rolled her eyes at Emma. "He is such a mess," she said in her most grown-up manner.

"No, Lizzie, he's probably hungry," Emma reminded her.

"I don't ever want a baby, that's for sure," Lizzie said as the wails continued from the bedroom.

"Lizzie, I mean it," Emma scolded.

Rachel came running up the stairs. She asked Mam if she could take Jason for a while. Mam handed him over gratefully, and Rachel walked the floor, bouncing him lightly up and down. He slowly quieted as she walked the floor, her strong arms carrying him back and forth. She stopped to watch the girls' game, and Lizzie could see she noticed Emma's dirty nightgown and wrinkled pillowcase and sheet.

"Lizzie, would you lay Baby Jason down a while? Over here on the rocker, and I'll get Emma all cleaned up and fix her couch all up with clean sheets. Would you like that, Emma? Come, and we'll give you a nice hot bath and wash your hair. Lizzie, do you know where Mam's clean sheets are? Could you get one for me?"

Emma was whisked into the bathroom, and Lizzie could hear Rachel talking softly as she washed Emma's hair.

Lizzie ran to the bedroom to ask Mam where the clean sheets were. Mandy was sound asleep on Mam's bed, and Mam was sitting on her rocking chair, crying.

Lizzie stopped and stared, her face changing from an expression of eager anticipation of helping Rachel to one of dismay. "Mam," Lizzie whispered.

"Oh, Lizzie, don't worry about me. I'm just a big baby. Jason just cries so much, the house is a mess, and I don't feel very good," Mam said tiredly.

Suddenly Lizzie blurted out, "Mam, I wish we wouldn't have Jason. He's so grouchy and you are crying because he isn't even cute—I know you are!"

Mam stared at Lizzie. Suddenly her tears changed to hysterical laughing. Actually, she was still crying, Lizzie thought, but laughing at the same time.

Lizzie didn't know what to do or say, so she stood by the doorway and stared at Mam, because it almost frightened her. Poor Mam. Lizzie was really glad Jason wasn't her baby.

Mam wiped her eyes and sighed a shaky sigh. "Come, Lizzie. I'll get some clean sheets and we'll make Emma a clean nest on the couch. I'm almost embarrassed to let Rachel see how things look around here this morning." She walked slowly over to the dresser and got sheets out of a drawer.

As they walked together, Lizzie laid her head against Mam. She wanted to comfort her somehow, but she didn't really know what to say. Mam's arm circled her shoulder and squeezed. "You're my Lizzie," Mam said with a smile. Lizzie felt so much better. She thought they'd all be much happier without Jason, but if he was here, they may as well make the best of it together.

Rachel was teaching Emma a new song in the bathroom. Mam smiled again as Rachel sang.

"Brush, brush, brush your teeth,
   Morning, noon, and night;
   Up and down and 'round and 'round,
   Until they're nice and white."

When they emerged from the bathroom, Emma's cheeks were pink from the hot water. Her dark hair was so clean, they were all shiny on the top of her head. She had a clean pink nightgown on and a warm pair of white socks.

"Here you go—lie down again," Rachel said to Mam. And she proceeded to spread the clean sheets on the couch with efficient moves.

Mam winked at Lizzie. "Rachel, you are a wonder."

"Oh, no, I'm just doing my job. I am getting paid, you know. I'll start the Saturday cleaning now, so you try and get some sleep while Jason does," Rachel said.

She got the dust cloth, dust mop, broom, and other cleaning necessities from the kitchen. As Lizzie watched, and Emma lay down on her sweet-smelling clean sheets, Rachel dusted and swept. She emptied waste cans, scoured the bathtub, and cleaned every window and mirror she could find. She got a plastic bucket of hot vinegar water, and with a big old rag, she cleaned the hardwood floor in the living room. She even pulled the couch forward and washed underneath it, after she had picked up all the trash and toys she found.

Lizzie helped a little, putting some of the toys away and telling Rachel where the bucket was. But Rachel moved so fast, whistling and singing, that Lizzie was almost dizzy from watching her.

Rachel stopped to look at the clock. "Almost dinner-time, Lizzie. What do we want to eat?" she asked.

"We could have toasted cheese sandwiches," Lizzie offered.

"Alright," Rachel said. She spread butter on slices of bread, found the cheese in the refrigerator, and toasted them in the pan. She also opened a jar of vegetable soup, and they had saltine crackers, applesauce, and pickles.

After lunch, Rachel did dishes again, then finished the cleaning. She even waxed the kitchen floor after everything else was done. Lizzie thought their house had never looked so nice. When Mandy spilled her pretzels on the floor, Lizzie made her pick them up right away.

After the fresh-smelling laundry was brought in and put neatly into drawers, Rachel asked Mam what to make for supper.

"Oh, I almost forgot, Rachel. You don't need to make supper. Aunt Anna is bringing our supper this evening," Mam said.

"That's so nice. Well then, I'll probably have to get ready to go away, as I'm supposed to be ready by seven o'clock," Rachel said shyly.

When Rachel was ready to go away, Lizzie was dumbfounded. She couldn't say a word, she felt so shy. Rachel looked beautiful in her good clothes when she was all dressed up. Lizzie didn't talk to her anymore — it was too scary. And when a horse and buggy stopped outside, Rachel's eyes sparkled and she smiled quickly.

"Thank you," she said as Mam handed the day's wages to her. "I'll be back on Monday morning. Will you be alright over Sunday?"

"Oh, yes, Rachel. You go enjoy yourself and don't worry about us for one minute. You have done so much, I feel like a different person. You are the best "maud" ever," Mam beamed.

"Just doing my job," Rachel smiled back.

"Now you'll have to tell us who is in that horse and buggy waiting for you," Mam said.

"You'll have to wait till Monday," Rachel said, and dashed down the stairs to the waiting buggy.

Lizzie was so thrilled. Imagine that, she thought. Someday, when she was as old as Rachel, she would act exactly like her. She'd look so pretty, and dash mysteriously down the stairs like Cinderella in her storybook. She might not have black hair, but Mam's wasn't black, either, and she was married.

She supposed some boys liked brown hair, too.

chapter 16

Going to Church

Baby Jason was almost three months old now. He was no longer red in color, and Lizzie thought he was actually looking a lot better. For one thing, he was growing more hair, and it looked as if they might be a bit curly. He also quit his screaming and crying, and Mam was not so tired. She sang while she washed dishes, and Rachel did not come to do the laundry, either. Lizzie missed her, but she knew Rachel would not always be their "maud."

So Lizzie decided she might have babies of her own someday, after all.

It was a fine spring morning, and it was Sunday. It was not the Glick family's regular church Sunday, but they were going to church at Grandpa Glicks, far away in another district. Lizzie did not have to wear her white cape and apron as usual. She was allowed to wear her

black Sunday one, because they were going to stay for
supper. If Mam didn't get too tired and Jason didn't cry
too much, they might even stay for the singing.

The singing was where the youth group, from the age
of sixteen until they married, gathered in the evening,
usually at the place where services were held during the
day.

Emma was excited to go to a different church district. She was much better and didn't need to stay on
the couch anymore. She still rested a lot, but she went
to school again, staying indoors with Teacher Sylvia at
recess.

Red trotted steadily down the road, his head held
high, as usual, and his trotting was fancy. In the buggy,
Emma and Lizzie sat in the back seat, with their black
woolen shawls tucked firmly around them. They could
not look out the back window, because the canvas
flap was fastened securely with snaps to keep out the
cold spring air. If the back window was open, and Dat
opened the front window to drive, the air blew strongly
through the buggy. So they kept it closed.

As they drove into Grandpa Glicks' lane, there were
lots of buggies parked along the driveway and close
to the barn. More buggies came from the other direction. Black horses, brown ones, big, beautiful ones, and
small, fat ones—all of them were interesting to Lizzie.
She loved horses and ponies, and going to a different
church gave Lizzie a chance to see lots of new horses.
She wished she wouldn't have to go into the house with
Mam and Emma. She'd much rather stay with Dat in

the barn, but that would not be proper.

So she hurried in the cleanly-swept sidewalk behind Mam, who was carrying Jason. Emma followed with a large plastic container which held the chocolate cake Mam had made yesterday. It was a layer cake, with fluffy white frosting between the chocolate layers. Lizzie was not allowed to have one bite, because you didn't take a cake to church that had already been cut.

They all went into the kettle house, where other women and girls were taking off their shawls and bonnets. Lizzie just stood in a corner, because she felt really shy. She didn't know very many people, especially not the little girls.

Suddenly someone tugged her bonnet string. "Hi, Lizzie. How are you?" beamed Aunt Barbie. "Do you want me to help you take off your shawl and bonnet?"

"Yes," Lizzie said softly.

She saw Elsie make her way through the crowded room. She squeezed Lizzie's hand and whispered, "Hi!" Lizzie smiled warmly at Elsie. "Hi," she whispered back.

Elsie said, "I'm so glad you came to church. Are you going to stay for supper and the singing?"

Emma joined them with her covering put neatly on her head. Little girls wore coverings just like their mothers did to go to church. Lizzie thought Emma looked really pretty, with her neat dark hair combed back in sleek rolls.

"Elsie, I think we're going to stay for the singing," Emma said.

"Are you?" Elsie smiled at Emma.

"I think so."

"I hope!" Elsie said.

Mam bustled over with Lizzie's covering. "Here, Lizzie." She held her chin, smoothed back her hair, and took the straight pins out of the covering. She held them between her lips as she put Lizzie's covering on her head. That always made Lizzie nervous. She wished Mam wouldn't do that, because suppose she swallowed them? She would have to go to the hospital and have an operation to get those pins out—Lizzie just knew it. So she watched Mam's mouth anxiously until the last pin was put in her covering.

Mandy was next, and Mam put those pins in her mouth, too. She didn't swallow them, either, and Lizzie sighed with relief.

Mam herded them all into the warm kitchen where the women were gathered. It was noisy with different conversations, as they talked about everyday occurrences.

Everything in the kitchen was sparkling clean. Grandma Glick was a hard worker, and her house was always clean, but when church was there it sparkled. The black gas stove was so shiny, Lizzie could see her reflection in the oven door. The stainless steel teakettle shone from being polished. The blue kitchen floor had little dark blue specks in it, and caught the sun's reflection with a fresh coat of wax.

Loaves of homemade bread in plastic bags were lined up on the counter. There were stacks of dishes on the countertop beside the big white refrigerator. Those were to put the pickles, red beets, cheese, and bologna on, Lizzie thought. Stacks of tablecloths and tea towels were all ready beside the dishes. Lizzie wondered where the snitz pies were. Snitz pies are dried apple pies, and they always had them in church.

Grandma Glick shook Lizzie's hand warmly, and next Emma's and Mandy's. "So glad you could come today," she smiled at Mam. "How is Jason doing now?"

"Oh, he's a lot better. I still think he simply had a touch of colic. It didn't matter what we tried, he just got those spells that he screamed because his little stomach hurt, I think."

"Yes," Grandma wisely nodded her head. "I know how that can be. With Marvin, he just kind of had to outgrow it."

She turned and stood at attention as the door opened and the ministers entered. Grandpa Glick was the first one because he was the oldest and also because he lived here. They all shook hands solemnly, and the women did not talk so much when the ministers came to shake hands.

Lizzie and Emma smiled up at Grandpa. He smiled down at them and squeezed their hands warmly. He didn't say anything because this was church. Maybe later in the afternoon he would.

After the ministers were seated in the big living room, Grandma showed the ministers' wives where to sit. There was plenty of room for everyone, because most of the furniture had been taken out of the house, or moved into the bedroom. Long wooden benches were set in

rows the evening before, and that is where everyone sat.
First the men filed in with their little boys. Sometimes
daughters sat with their fathers, and today Lizzie knew
she would have to, because Emma would sit with Mam
and Jason in the kitchen with the other relatives. Lizzie
didn't really want to because she was seven now. But
she knew Mandy was more well-behaved with Dat, so
when they saw Dat come in, Lizzie took Mandy's hand
and walked over to him. He took her hand, and they
found a seat on a bench along the wall.

There was a strange-looking man sitting beside
Lizzie, and he had two strange-looking boys. His hair
was very long and very black, as was his beard. His
eyebrows were long and bushy, with piercing blue eyes
underneath, and he looked a bit scary to Lizzie. When
he coughed, Lizzie almost jumped off the bench. It was
a loud, raspy sound that didn't sound like Dat's cough.
His boys were wriggling around on the bench, trying
to take their coats off. He didn't help them, and Lizzie

guessed he was mean to them. She looked at Dat for re-
assurance, but he was talking quietly with Uncle James.

Lizzie moved as close to Dat as she could and put one
hand under Dat's arm. He felt her touch, and looked
down at her and smiled. Lizzie felt a bit better, but she
kept casting glances at the strange man. He looked like a
man in a war book that Lizzie had seen once.

Someone picked a song, saying the number in German. Dat found the page and soon the room was filled
with the sound of the slow German singing. Usually
Lizzie enjoyed that, but for some reason, she felt like
crying today. She had a lump in her throat, and a wave
of genuine sadness washed over her. She blinked and
tried to think happy thoughts, or at least something
funny. She thought about the afternoon, when church
was over, and they could play with Marvin, but that
didn't make her feel better at all.

She felt the man beside her move quickly. Lizzie saw
him reach over and pinch one of his little boys as hard as
he could. He twisted the boy's arm, talking to him quite
sternly. The little boy opened his mouth and let out a
crying howl of pain and surprise.

Lizzie blinked and put her hand under Dat's arm. Dat
looked over at the howling little boy, but looked away
again to be polite. Lizzie sat and looked straight ahead,
trying not to watch him cry. His father did not try to
comfort him or make him feel better. He was singing
loudly as his little boy wailed beside him.

Lizzie had the blues. She was so afraid of that strange
man, and Dat was singing as if nothing was wrong at all.

She felt more and more dejected, even if she knew she
was much too old to cry in church.

Her nose started to run, so she got out her little flowered handkerchief and carefully wiped her nose. Even
before tears formed, a sob tore at her throat. Dat looked
down at Lizzie. He put his arm around her, bent low,
and whispered, "What's wrong, Lizzie?"

With Dat's kindness, her blues dissolved into tears,
and she sobbed quietly. She hid her face in Dat's "mut-
sa," or suit coat, and cried. He patted her shoulder, and
asked her again why she was crying. Lizzie couldn't
tell him, because maybe it was just herself, and she was
acting like a baby. But she really did not like that black-
haired man and his little boy.

So Dat just kept his arm around her and let her cry
quietly.

Lizzie felt a bit better after she was finished crying,
so Dat let her put her head on his leg, and she relaxed.
She thought of snitz pie and cheese bread and wished
it was time for church to be over. She was thinking of
people who put peanut butter spread on their bread,
then cheese on top, and wondered why. When she fell
asleep, she dreamed she was eating peanut butter bread
and bologna, and the black-haired man took it from her
and dipped it in his coffee.

.   .   .   .   .

Church services were over and Lizzie, Emma, and
Elsie were watching Jason while their mothers hurried
back and forth, getting the long table ready, with tablecloths and dishes.

They spread the table with dried apple pies, cheese and bologna, dark green pickles, and pungent red beets. Shimmering grape jelly and homemade butter made the table look pretty. There was also a peanut butter spread made with molasses, marshmallow creme, and—of course—peanut butter.

The men and their little boys sat at one table, and the women and small girls sat at another. They all bowed their heads in silent prayer, and Lizzie, Elsie, and Emma had to hold perfectly still, too, even if they were not at the table. Lizzie never liked to do that, because if you were eating, you didn't know if you should chew quietly or just hold the food in your mouth and hold it very still. That was not easy to do, because you needed to chew food if it was in your mouth. *That is just the way a mouth is*, Lizzie thought.

After lunch Elsie told Emma that she was going to get Baby Eva, Aunt Sarah's baby girl. Emma could have Jason, and they would go upstairs to the aunts' bedrooms and play church with their babies.

Lizzie was hurt. "Well, who am I going to have? You both have a baby and I don't even have one," she pouted.

"You are almost too little, Lizzie," Elsie said kindly.

"You don't like babies very much, anyway. You know you don't," Emma added.

"I do."

"No, you don't, Lizzie. You say they always scratch your face. Besides, you can't carry a real baby up the stairs," Emma said, bossily.

"I can, too!" Lizzie shouted.

"Shhh! Not so loud," Emma hushed Lizzie.

"You always think you're the boss, Emma. I'm not going to play if I can't have a baby!" Lizzie yelled louder.

Marvin came hurrying over. "What is wrong?" he asked, looking closely at Lizzie's flushed face.

"We want to play church," Elsie sighed, "and Lizzie thinks she has to have her own baby or she won't play."

"I'll help," Marvin said. "I'll be the preacher, Lizzie, and you can be Elsie's child." He bent down closely and peered at Lizzie. "Okay?"

"No. That would look too dumb. I'm almost as big as Elsie. I don't want to be a child, anyway. I want to be a mother," Lizzie said firmly.

Marvin looked puzzled. Emma sighed and shifted Jason more comfortably on her lap.

Elsie said helplessly, "Well, I don't know what to do."

They all sat down and thought.

"I know!" Marvin jumped up. "Lizzie could be the preacher's wife. Then we'd be way too old to have a baby. I'd be an old doddy preacher and she could be the mommy."

Lizzie grinned. That sounded like fun, she and Marvin being an old couple, and she would have to sit way up front close to Marvin while he preached.

So they all agreed, and Marvin set the small benches, where they assembled themselves in solemn order. Emma played quietly with Jason while they sang. It didn't sound exactly right, but it sounded close to what they heard in church. Lizzie sat up straight and sang as

loud as she could, until Elsie glanced at her with a questioning look. At the same time, Emma poked her hard in
the side of her apron, and pricked her finger on a pin.

"Ouch!" she cried.

They all fell into a helpless fit of giggles, and the only
person singing was Marvin. He turned around to glare
at them in exasperation. "Now, I mean it, you have to
play right. This is not fun if you don't act real!"

The girls were still laughing, with Baby Jason laughing along with them.

"Oh, don't be so strict, Marvin," Elsie said after she
caught her breath.

Lizzie felt sorry for Marvin, so she told everyone to
act more real, because, after all, Marvin was the preacher. So when Marvin stood up and cleared his throat,
tugging at his black vest, the girls sat up and listened, a
very serious expression on their upturned faces.

Marvin preached loud and long. Emma got her
wrinkled little handkerchief and wiped her eyes, sniffing
with emotion.

Lizzie thought Marvin actually was a good preacher.
He said lots of serious things that real preachers said,
except he didn't say very many big German words like a
real preacher did. That was alright, because Lizzie didn't
understand them anyway.

.   .   .   .   .

Later that evening, when the youth came to sing,
Lizzie was getting really tired. They had all played
together, and there was so much good food to eat, that
Lizzie's eyes were getting heavy while they waited for

the youth to start the singing.

Just when she thought she would have to give up and tell Mam she wanted to lie on Grandma's bed, the buggies started coming in the drive.

When the kettle house door opened and Rachel was the first girl to enter the kitchen, Lizzie's heart skipped a beat. There was Rachel! Lizzie wanted to run over and hug her and hold her hand, but there were too many other girls with her. She was too shy. So she sat on her chair and watched her beloved Rachel shake hands with all the people in the kitchen.

When Rachel came to Emma and Lizzie, she swooped them up in a warm hug. Lizzie hugged her back and smiled happily; it felt so good to be with Rachel again. "Hi, Rachel!" was all Lizzie could think to say.

"Hello, girls—it's so good to see you again. I thought you would probably be here tonight," Rachel beamed. She had to move on so that the other girls could take their place at the table.

They all started singing German songs from a songbook. The boys soon followed, and the volume increased as the boys joined in. Lizzie, Elsie, and Emma sat side by side, watching very closely how everyone looked, and listening to the wonderful singing. Lizzie liked it better than the church songs, because the tunes were faster. On some songs, Lizzie felt like tapping her feet in time to the music. She didn't, though, because that would not have been proper. She wished she could, though.

On their way home, late in the evening, Lizzie, Emma, and Mandy were snuggled cozily under a woolen blanket in the dark, rumbling buggy. Under the seat was the leftover chocolate cake, a bowl of tapioca pudding, and two snitz pies that Grandma Glick had sent along home.

Dat and Mam were discussing the day's events, and Lizzie wondered which one was Rachel's boyfriend, then she fell sound asleep on Emma's shoulder.

Summertime

School was over! Emma and Lizzie came home on the last day of school with their report cards that said they were promoted to second grade. The only reason they knew what it said was because Lavina Lapp told them it meant they had passed.

Dat and Mam praised the girls for having made it through first grade. Dat said they must have worked hard, but Lizzie didn't really know why he said that, because school was not hard. She could read lots of other books besides her reading book at school, and she spelled third grade spelling words. So she supposed Dat didn't know that, and she didn't tell him.

The days were getting warmer, and they were allowed to go barefoot. Dat opened the windows in the harness shop, and the warm, sweet summer air blew through them, giving the shop a new fragrance. He was always busy, waiting on customers or sewing at the big sewing machine, whistling or singing as he worked.

Lizzie loved to feel the smooth, oily feeling of the warm brown wooden floor on her feet. She swept the shop with a big bristly broom that you pushed, but she was too small to do a very good job. So she just stayed with Dat, asking questions or listening to him talk with customers who came to order harnesses or buy a pair of shoes.

When Emma came running down the stairs, shouting for Lizzie, she just knew she had something bossy to say. And sure enough, Emma told Lizzie loudly that as soon as Mam was done washing, they had to help mow the yard, trim around the flower beds, and make new flower beds today.

Lizzie didn't feel like working in the yard. Emma just upset her, always spoiling a perfect day, telling her what she had to do. So she didn't turn around. She acted as if she didn't hear Emma, just keeping her back turned.

"Lizzie!" Emma was upset; Lizzie could tell by how loud she was. Good for her; she could go mow the yard with Mam and she'd stay here with Dat.

"Lizzie!" Emma yelled louder.

Dat stopped his sewing machine and looked at the girls. He did not look very happy when he turned Lizzie around. "Lizzie, answer your sister when she calls you," he said firmly. Lizzie looked at the floor, pushing a piece of black leather with one toe.

"Dat, you have to make Lizzie listen to me. She's just mad because she has to work. I already swept the floor for Mam and she didn't do a thing," Emma snorted.

"Lizzie, now go on, and don't be so stubborn," Dat said, giving her a shove. He looked frustrated, and turned back to his sewing machine.

"I don't want to, and I'm not . . ." Lizzie retorted.

Dat got up very suddenly and loomed over Lizzie. "Don't say it, Lizzie, or I'm going to have to find my paddle. You go right now and be nice. I'm busy here and Mam needs you to help her. Now go."

Lizzie burst into howls of rage and disappointment. First of all, Emma was bossy, and now Dat was on Emma's side and was being so unkind. So she wailed her way out the door and plopped down hard on the porch step, refusing to budge, amid loud howls of self-pity.

"Lizzie, if you don't shut up right this minute — oh!" Emma stood helplessly, and when she couldn't take Lizzie's crying one more second, she stomped off to the little shed and found the push mower.

Lizzie could hardly cry anymore because she was watching Emma mow. It looked like fun, and it made the lawn look nice and even in size and color. She sniffed and wiped her eyes and watched Emma some more. She watched two butterflies chase each other over Emma's head, and a pigeon swooped down to sit on a branch of the apple tree.

Lizzie felt bad inside. It was so nice and warm, and the sun shone with a soft yellow glow, but it didn't help Lizzie feel better at all. She wished she could go to school. School was much more fun than this. She just knew how her whole summer would be, with Emma

bossing her around. Mandy was too little to be much
fun, but she guessed if Emma was going to be so grown-
up all the time, sweeping floors and mowing yard,
Mandy would have to do. Even Dat was unkind to her
today.

Emma stopped the mower and wiped her face with
the skirt of her dress. "Emma, put your dress down,"
Lizzie said angrily.

"Lizzie, you know what? You cannot keep acting
this way. Mam says we can't go to Heaven if we aren't
good girls, and you have to learn to give up. You're old
enough," Emma said firmly.

"How do you know?" Lizzie asked, kicking at a crack
in the porch step. She pulled out a strand of hair from
her bob, and yanked at it. Tears welled up in her eyes,
because it hurt dreadfully. She turned away so Emma
couldn't see, and ran to the toolshed. She found Mam's
trimming shears, and hurried over to the flower bed
farthest away from Emma.

She clipped halfheartedly at the edge of the flower
bed. A fat brown earthworm wriggled in the grass, and
Lizzie clipped him in two pieces. It served the slimy old
worm right—he had no business crawling over the grass
where she was supposed to trim.

Mam came over and sat down beside Lizzie. The two
parts of the earthworm were wriggling furiously, and
Mam could see Lizzie's swollen eyes and tear-stained
face. She watched Emma mowing yard with her nose a
bit higher than necessary and guessed the whole usual
scene of her two oldest girls. Mam sighed.

"What's wrong with the worm, Lizzie?" she asked
kindly.

"I cut him in half."

"On purpose?" Mam asked.

"I don't know."

"Lizzie, why were you crying?" she asked, kind as
always.

"Mam, I–I—" and Lizzie burst into a fresh wave of
weeping. "It's always the same. Emma is so good and I
am so bad. She always makes me do things I don't want
to, because she likes to sweep and do things like that.
And she makes me so mad I could . . . I could kick her.
And you like her a lot better than you like me. Dat does,
too."

Mam watched the light green leaves on the apple tree fluttering in the breeze. She looked down at her second daughter's angry little face, and at the worm she had cut in her frustration. Mam sighed and dug the toe of her shoe into the grass.

This is not going to be easy, she thought. *I do believe Lizzie is a more complex little person than we think. How can we help her learn to give up?*

"Lizzie." Mom cleared her throat.

"What?" Lizzie looked up, swiping a hand across her cheeks that were smeared with dirt. She tucked a stray hair behind her ears, and pulled at a hairpin in her bob.

"You know that's not true. Dat would never love one of his daughters more than the other. Do you think I would? Truthfully?" Mam asked kindly.

She turned to reach out to Lizzie, but her daughter pulled away. So Mam decided it was not the time or place to teach Lizzie about giving up and doing something she didn't want to do.

"Let's all work hard, Lizzie—okay? Then we'll make a big cold pitcher of grape Kool-Aid and we'll make popcorn with lots of butter. And Dat can help you ride your pony."

"No." Lizzie was still pouting.

"Alright, then. Emma and I will do it alone." Mam jumped up and started trimming, pulling weeds as she went.

Lizzie watched Emma mowing. She looked so warm and tired, and she was skipping some grass. It wasn't cut nice and straight, because there were thin rows of grass still standing. Without thinking, Lizzie hurried over to Emma. "You're not getting all the grass." She pointed to a skipped piece.

"What?" Emma was hot and tired, and Lizzie had just finished her desire to mow. "Okay, then—you do it." And she stalked off.

So Lizzie began to mow. She was almost too little, but she loved to feel the power of making the sharp reels go around, cutting the grass in an even row. She marched back and forth, back and forth, and forgot all her troubles. This was really fun. She would love to help Mam all summer long, she thought.

After a while, the sun felt very warm. Sweat ran down her back, and felt like it was oozing out of her head. But she kept mowing, watching Mam and Emma working in the flower beds. She bet anything Mam thought she could really mow the yard well for as small as she was.

She hit a bump, and the handle of the mower hit her chest, hard. She stopped to wipe her forehead with the hem of her dress, glancing quickly over her shoulder to make sure Emma didn't see her, because she'd tell Lizzie to put her dress down.

Mandy was playing in the sandbox, happily mixing gravel, sand, and water. Lizzie walked over to see what she was doing. Mam hurried past, on her way to check on Jason, who was taking a nap.

Lizzie sat on the edge of the sandbox, watching a row of ants parading along the edge of the gravel. Emma came over with a bucket of weeds to dump in the mulch pile.

"Lizzie, if you would help, we could soon ride our pony," she offered kindly.

"What do you want me to do?" Lizzie asked.

"Well, I think Mam said we can go as soon as that one flower bed is cleaned."

Lizzie wrinkled her nose.

"Maybe Jason will wake up and Mam won't come out again," she told Emma.

Dat opened the screen door and called to the girls, "If you go get Dolly out, I'll help you put the saddle on her. I'm getting really tired, and since it's so nice outside, I can hardly work in here today."

"Oh, goody!" They raced to the barn, scattering gravel with every step. Lizzie yanked open the wooden door, and the sweet coolness of the barn's interior felt so good. Dolly's nicker sounded from the pen along the back. She put her head over the bars of the gate, nickering again.

"Emma! Emma!" Dat's call turned their heads in the direction of the house. Lizzie ran to the door and shouted back as loud as she could. "What?"

"Lizzie, don't get Dolly now. Mam made popcorn and a cold drink. Come, and we'll sit on the grass a while," Dat called.

Lizzie turned to Emma. "Emma, don't get her out now. Mam made popcorn," she said.

"Okay." Emma raced Lizzie to the yard. They plopped down in the fresh green grass and lay on their stomachs, kicking their bare feet in the air, and pulling short pieces of grass out by the roots.

Mandy joined them, carrying a big plastic bowl of

freshly popped corn. Dat was behind her, carrying a
pitcher filled with ice-cold Kool-Aid. Mam hurried behind him, carrying Jason and a tall stack of glasses.

They all sat in the grass, enjoying their cold drinks.
Jason waved his arms and gurgled his baby gurgles,
while Mandy threw handfuls of popcorn in the air, until
Dat made her stop.

Dat helped Mam put away the gardening tools and
the lawn mower, while Emma and Lizzie got Dolly out
of her pen. They brushed her mane and tail until they
were completely untangled. Then they used a firm cur-
rycomb and rubbed her coat until she shone.

"She's the prettiest pony in the whole world," Lizzie
said proudly. She stood back and admired Dolly, and
the pony gave her tail a saucy little flick.

"Come on, Lizzie, you carry the saddle. Let's go. Dat's
going to help us." Emma was on her way out the door,
leading Dolly. Lizzie stooped to get the saddle. It was
really heavy, but she managed, although she had to be
very careful not to trip over the stirrups.

Dat met them in the yard, and after talking to Dolly
in his pony talk, he eased the saddle onto her back.
Emma watched every move he made, taking note of
how he pulled the straps tight and how he knotted them.
Lizzie pitied Dolly. Dat yanked too hard on the girth,
she thought, and the poor pony's stomach was certainly
not comfortable.

"Dat?" she said quietly.

"Hmmm?"

"Are you sure that band around Dolly's stomach isn't

too tight? I mean, how would you like to run with a band around your stomach so tight?" she asked.

Dat's laugh rang out. He put two fingers between Dolly's stomach and the band that went around it. "Oh, Lizzie, if you can only find something to worry about! It's really not as tight as it seems. Feel it."

So Lizzie put her hand where Dat showed her, but she was still doubtful. It felt tight.

Emma was allowed to ride first. Dat helped her into the saddle, showing her how to place her feet correctly into the stirrups. He led Dolly for a while, until Emma felt brave enough to ride her on her own. She trotted Dolly down the gravel driveway, as Dat stood and watched. When Emma turned Dolly and trotted back to Dat, he was smiling.

"Very good, Emma. I think you can handle Dolly well enough to ride her on your own. I'm going to the shop for a minute; I see a customer just pulled in. Let Lizzie have a turn. I'll be right back." Dat hurried into the shop.

Lizzie held Dolly's bridle, and looked up at Emma. "Get off now, Emma. It's my turn," she said.

"Not yet, Lizzie."

"Yes. Dat said. Now get off."

Dolly shook her head up and down. She was getting impatient—Lizzie just knew it.

"Just let me ride her around the yard once, Lizzie. Then I'll let you, okay?" Emma asked.

"Oh, okay. You always get your own way anyhow." And Lizzie stepped aside, so Dolly could go.

Emma picked up the reins and clicked her tongue. Dolly lifted her head and started off at a lively pace. Around and around the yard Dolly trotted. Lizzie was getting more and more impatient.

And then things happened so fast, Lizzie couldn't even remember later how it all was. First she remembered hearing a loud, rattling sound. Then it was all a blur. A team of two huge workhorses pulling a steel-wheeled wagon with a load of other farm implements rattled into sight. Dolly was trotting along and was suddenly startled by the wagon and horses. Up, up, she went, rearing up with her front legs off the ground.

Emma's high-pitched scream of terror jolted Lizzie into action. She started running toward Dolly. Her first thought was to help Emma somehow.

Directly under a sturdy branch, Dolly veered to the left, and Emma pitched to the right. Emma's hair caught on the knobby branch, and she was suspended from it, while Dolly ran out from underneath her.

Emma screamed and cried. Lizzie yelled and yelled for Dat. She was crying and screaming hoarsely while Emma swung from the branch by her hair.

Just as Dat appeared, running across the porch, Emma's hair tore loose from her head and she fell to the grass below. She lay in a pitiful heap, her hand pressed to the place where her hair had been torn.

Lizzie reached Emma first, and dropped down on her knees beside her. Dat soon followed, and he took Emma's hands away from her head. He was terrified, Lizzie could tell, and she started crying louder than ever. This was so awful, Lizzie couldn't even think of anything except to cry as loud as she could.

"Emma!" Dat said very loudly in an awful voice. "What happened?"

Emma was crying hysterically. Lizzie just cried with her, because it looked so horrible, and she was so afraid Emma was going to die, with her hair pulled out so cruelly.

"I–I–I—" Emma wailed.

Lizzie swallowed. "Dat, Dat." She tried to tell him what happened, but all she could do was cough and hiccup and cry some more.

Dat pulled Emma close, holding her and rocking back and forth. He pulled out his handkerchief and pressed it to the side of Emma's head where blood and water oozed out of the bald spot where Emma's beautiful, shiny, dark hair had been.

"Dat." Lizzie took a deep breath to steady herself. She began bravely, drawing in another deep breath. "Dat, Emma wanted another turn around the yard and that . . . that rattly wagon went past and scared Dolly."

Dat nodded his head.

"And . . . and then, she reared way up, Dat, and Emma . . . Emma—" and Lizzie burst into fresh sobs.

Dat held Emma close and reached for Lizzie. "Come here, Lizzie. My goodness."

And Lizzie crumpled beside Dat on the soft green grass and his strong arm held her close against him. His hands were black and smelled of harnesses and grease. His soft beard touched the top of Lizzie's head, and it was the most comforting touch she had ever felt. Dat was so safe and so strong, that everything was not quite so terrible anymore.

She peeped around to Emma. *Poor Emma,* Lizzie thought. She was in terrible pain. Her face was so white, and she was shaking all over. Dat just sat and held the girls while Emma calmed down.

"Lizzie," Dat said quietly, "would you go ask Mam for some peroxide to put on Emma's head? And ask her to come here for a minute."

So Lizzie went to find Mam. She was folding clothes at the kitchen table, quite unaware of anything that had happened.

"Mam," Lizzie called.

"Hmm?" Mam didn't even look up; she was busy.

"Dat asked you to come and bring some peroxide," said Lizzie.

Mam looked up. She looked at Lizzie more carefully. "Why? Lizzie, what happened? Were you crying?" she asked.

"Yes, I was, Mam. Emma got caught in the apple tree and was swinging by her hair, and . . . it . . . it tore out."

"Lizzie! You stop that! You know that's not true." Mam was very upset with Lizzie.

"Mam! It is true. Come with me," Lizzie said, all upset again because Mam would not believe her.

So Mam went to the bathroom and got the peroxide, scooped up Jason, and with Mandy following, they hurried down the stairs, and over to Dat and Emma.

"Melvin, what in the world is wrong?" With a cry of

alarm, Mam fell to her knees beside Emma and held her
close. Fresh tears squeezed out of Emma's closed eyes,
as she laid her head against Mam's apron. Mam's hands
felt Emma's head, and she gasped as she took away
Dat's handkerchief.

"Melvin! You mean . . . ?" She spread her hands in a
gesture of helplessness.

"Yes, it happened just like Lizzie said."

"Melvin, you have to stop leaving the girls alone with
this pony. Just look what happened." Mam's voice rose
to a high-pitched exclamation of dismay.

"I'm sorry. I just never thought it wouldn't be safe.
Dolly is so used to the girls, and listens so well to them, I
just thought I could wait on this customer, and they'd be
alright." Dat felt very bad.

Mam carefully patted peroxide on Emma's wound.
Emma winced, but Mam was so gentle she didn't say
anything.

Lizzie looked around and sighed. How could a perfect
summer afternoon become so scary? Even the butterflies
and the birds in the apple tree looked scary. Anything
could happen. She shivered. She pulled in her lower lip
and bit down hard. Life just was that way. It was scary,
because you never knew what could happen. But, in
spite of it all, she was so glad that Emma did not die.
Bossy or not, she would miss Emma very, very much
and always wish she had helped her sweep the kitchen.

chapter 18

A Trip to Ohio

Because it was summer, Emma and Lizzie did not have to go to school. So now Dat and Mam decided that it would be a good time to visit Doddy Millers in Ohio. Except Mam would have to go by herself, with Emma, Lizzie, Mandy, and Baby Jason, because Dat had to stay at home and work in the harness shop. He had lots of harnesses to repair, because the horses were working in the fields, and also, he had plenty of new ones to make as well. So Dat said Emma should be a big helper to Mam, because they were going by themselves.

Lizzie wondered why Dat didn't say anything to her. She could hold Mandy's hand and act every bit as grown-up as Emma. But Emma was older, she thought; that's how it always was.

Mam was very busy the week before they were supposed to leave. Dat got their tickets, and made arrangements for a driver to take them all to the train station in the big city. Mam sewed some new short-sleeved dresses for the girls to wear, and she made new pants and shirts for Jason. She sang as she worked, and Lizzie could tell Mam was excited. Lizzie was, too, because she only remembered a little bit about her first train ride when she was small.

When the driver pulled up to the porch that fine summer morning, everybody was all dressed up and ready to go. Dat helped them all into the van, stowing the suitcases in the back. Mam made sure the doors were locked before she hurried out to sit beside Emma in the first seat. Dat sat on the front seat with the driver.

Lizzie and Emma chattered excitedly. Lizzie told Emma that the best part of this whole trip was the train ride. Emma thought the best part was being at Doddy Millers.

"I know," Lizzie agreed, "but when you ride on a train, you can see much more. All the English people and their fancy shoes, the big tall buildings in the cities, and it's much more exciting than just being at Doddy Millers."

"Lizzie," Emma said, quite seriously.

"What?"

"You shouldn't be quite so wild in your mind. Why do you have to look at all the fancy shoes, anyway?" Emma asked her.

"Oh, they just look pretty. Especially the white ones with

high heels. If I'd be English, that is exactly what I would wear. They make a nice clicking noise, too," Lizzie said.

Emma said nothing, so Lizzie folded her hands in her lap and thought Emma agreed with her. She looked down at her own navy-colored sneakers that had a white sole on them, and thought she had nice shoes for an Amish girl. She was happy with her new lavender-colored dress with a black apron. She liked being Amish — she just liked to watch fancy ladies with high heels. Emma just didn't understand that.

Dat and the driver were talking, and Mam was smiling and humming under her breath. Lizzie thought Mam must surely be happy and excited, because her eyes were sparkling and she just smiled and smiled.

When they arrived at the train station, it was almost time for their train. Dat helped them with their luggage, and they sat on soft red chairs that you could hardly stay on. Lizzie had to push her feet hard against the leg, or she would have slid off. Lizzie wished they had chairs like that at home, because she and Emma would have lots of fun pushing each other off the seats.

A loud voice boomed from a corner of the ceiling. Lizzie and Emma jumped, because it was so loud.

"There we are," Dat said, as a crowd of people turned to look at blinking letters above one exit. "Hold tight to my hand," Dat told Lizzie. "Emma, you take Mandy's."

So Lizzie put her hand in Dat's big, warm, safe one, and they all moved forward with the rest of the crowd. A long, low whistle sounded, and Lizzie's arms felt prickly, like they did when she was cold. She heard a click-clacking noise, and tears welled in her eyes. It was all so loud and strange, it just made her feel like crying. When the huge engine came into sight, with all the lights blinking and the shiny metal glowing in the morning sun, Lizzie was so excited that she bit her lip so hard she tasted blood. She still felt like crying, and her nose was running, so she wiped her face hard on her sleeve and sniffed.

Dat looked around to make sure they were all there. He smiled at Lizzie, to reassure her that everything would be fine. Mam stood beside them, her blue dress blowing out from the rush of the train's passing. Her cheeks were flushed, and her eyes sparkled, while she held Jason tightly with one arm, and the navy blue suitcase was clutched tightly in the other. Her purse was slung across one shoulder. Emma and Mandy held on to the same handle, so they would not get lost in the crowd.

When the train stopped, a dark-skinned man stepped down and shouted, "All aboard! All aboard for Winesburg!" He wore a brown and beige uniform, with a cap on his head that had letters on it, but Lizzie didn't know what it said. She guessed maybe it said something about sandwiches, because when she was younger, on her first train ride, a black man came down the aisle with a big tray of sandwiches, and Mam bought one for her. Lizzie hoped it was the same man, and Mam would buy her another sandwich.

Mam looked at Dat, squeezed his hand, and told him goodbye. Dat hugged all three of the girls in one big, enveloping hug, and there were tears in his eyes as he said,

"Goodbye, girls. Come home again as soon as you can. I'll take good care of Dolly until you come home." With a final pat, he smiled, and they all went up the bumpy metal steps into the train.

Mam found a seat for Emma and Lizzie, and found another seat beside them, across the aisle. She put her purse and small suitcase on the floor, but the large suitcase she lifted to a rack above their heads. Lizzie was glad Mam was so strong, because who else would have lifted that heavy suitcase? Mam was brave, too, or else she wouldn't go on the train with all the children. Lizzie was glad she had a mother like that.

A man with white hair was watching Mam put away her suitcase. He leaned around the corner of the seat, and said quietly, "Ma'am, I could have done that for you."

"Oh, no, that would not have been necessary. It really was not that heavy. Thank you just the same," she said, and smiled.

"Well, you certainly are a brave lady. Are these all your children?" he inquired.

"Yes, they are," Mam said. "This is Jason and Mandy, and Emma and Lizzie are seated across the aisle."

"Beautiful children. Beautiful," the white-haired man beamed.

Mam looked shy, but she said quietly, "Thank you."

Lizzie was so glad the man said they were beautiful. She bet he meant it. It was because of her navy sneakers with white soles, and her new lavender dress. Lizzie clasped her hands tightly and sighed happily, sitting up straight. This was so much fun, she could hardly sit still for a minute. Emma was just as thrilled, Lizzie could tell, because she was wriggling around in her seat, trying to look out the window at the train station.

"Emma, you can't see Dat anymore, can you?" Lizzie asked.

Emma hopped up on her knees to look out the window. She looked very carefully all around the train station before she shook her head. "No, Lizzie, he went home as soon as we got on the train," she said.

"Why aren't we moving?" Lizzie asked Emma.

"I don't know."

"Do you suppose there's something wrong with the train?" Lizzie asked anxiously.

"I hope not," Emma answered.

"Mam, why aren't we moving?" Lizzie asked, from across the aisle.

"Oh, they have things to load and unload first, I suppose. Why? Are you in a hurry to go to Doddys?" she asked.

"Of course!" Emma answered.

Mam arranged Jason more firmly on her lap and winked at Emma. "Me, too!" she said.

"Mam, are you going to buy me a sandwich from that black man?" Lizzie asked.

"Oh, we'll have to see. I do have some sandwiches and snacks packed in my bag for us to eat," she answered.

"Do, Mam. Those sandwiches are different than ours," Lizzie said.

Mam just smiled. Then she told the girls to look out the window, because the train was starting to move. And sure enough, when they looked out, the train station was slowly slipping away. It made Lizzie feel funny, because if you didn't focus your eyes right, it seemed as if the train was actually holding still, and it was the station that was moving. Lizzie and Emma looked at each other and giggled.

Faster and faster the train sped along the tracks. Buildings, trees, and telephone wires all became a blur through the window. The whole train swayed in little movements that made you slant a bit in your seat. Lizzie thought it must be hard to walk in the aisle, because the train was swaying from side to side.

Jason and Mandy soon fell asleep, the constant motion rocking them until they became sleepy. Mam rested her head on the back of the seat, and Emma and Lizzie relaxed.

"Emma, who do you think is going to meet us in Ohio at that train station?" Lizzie asked.

"Probably Doddy Miller. He did the last time," Emma said.

"Do you remember the last time?" Lizzie asked.

"Mm-hmm."

"Do you remember everything?"

"No, not everything. I just remember that Doddy came to meet us, and that he grabbed my neck with his cane like he usually does," Emma replied.

"Oh," Lizzie said.

After a while, Emma said she remembered Mommy

Miller made custard pies that were so good, she ate two big pieces.

"I don't remember," Lizzie said.

"That's because you were too little," Emma sniffed.

"Oh," said Lizzie.

A door opened at the end of their car, and the tall black man entered. He was talking in English to some of the passengers, so the girls didn't know what he was saying. Mam got her purse and took out two yellow pieces of paper. She held them carefully and when the black man came to Mam, he tipped his hat politely.

"How do you do, ma'am? Your tickets, please."

Mam handed them to him and smiled up at him. The black man punched the tickets with something that looked like Teacher Sylvia's hole puncher in school.

"There you are, ma'am. These all yours?" He looked at Emma and Lizzie, and for a moment, Lizzie felt his piercing look from his deep, very dark brown eyes. He smiled at them with his white teeth showing against his dark skin. Lizzie was fascinated by this man. She had never seen a person look so dark and shiny. She wondered why God made some people with dark skin and some with white. She looked down at her arms, and suddenly her skin seemed much too white. She wished her skin was as dark as the black man's skin, because it was prettier.

"Emma," she whispered.

"What?" Emma whispered back.

"How come he said 'Mam' to Mam? She's not his Mam," Lizzie said.

"He didn't," Emma said.

"Yes, he did. I heard him!" Lizzie shot back.

"Ask Mam."

So Lizzie leaned across the aisle and asked Mam why he called her "Mam."

Mam laughed. "Ach, Lizzie, your ears just don't miss a thing, do they?" she said.

"Well . . ." Lizzie started.

"No, he said 'ma'am', which is short for 'madam.' That's a polite way to address a woman. It's old-fashioned and really rather nice," she told Lizzie.

"Oh, I thought he said 'Mam,'" Lizzie replied.

The door opened again, and another black man appeared. He had a wide strap around his neck that was attached to a big square tray held against his stomach. On this tray were the sandwiches and drinks that Lizzie was hoping Mam would buy.

This man was short and a bit heavy. He joked and laughed as he sold things from the big tray.

"Mam?" Lizzie asked.

"Do you want a sandwich, Lizzie?" Mam asked.

"Emma and I can share, if they cost too much," Lizzie offered.

When the black man came to Mam, he asked her if she wanted anything. Lizzie held her breath as Mam reached down for her purse.

"Yes, I'll have two chicken salad sandwiches and two Cokes," she said.

Lizzie could hardly believe it. Mam was really nice and kind, buying those good things. Lizzie knew she had

packed food for their train ride, and this was just for a
special treat. She loved Mam so much right at that moment, because she was a kind, good Mam.

Emma and Lizzie had to be very careful, because the
train made a rolling motion. The black man opened the
glass bottle of soda for them, and put in two straws, one
for Lizzie, and one for Emma.

"There you go, sweeties." He smiled at the girls, and
Lizzie smiled back. She didn't really mean to smile, but
she was so happy with her chicken salad sandwich, she
just smiled before she thought about it.

The black man with the tray went whistling and jok-
ing down the aisle. Emma and Lizzie looked at each
other and giggled. They carefully sipped Coke from the
bottle. Tears formed in their eyes and their noses burned
because the soda was so bubbly. Lizzie burped out loud,
and clasped her hand across her mouth, her eyes wide
with surprise. Emma threw back her head and laughed,
but Mam frowned at Lizzie and told her to say, "Excuse
me."

Lizzie did, then they giggled some more. The chicken
salad had pieces of green celery and flaky white pieces
of chicken in it. Creamy mayonnaise was mixed with the
chicken, and put between soft white pieces of bread. The
sandwich wasn't cut straight across like Mam cut their
sandwiches for school. It was cut diagonally, and made
two perfect triangles. Lizzie thought it was fancy and it
made the sandwich taste even better. She savored every
bite of that delicious sandwich.

"Mam," she said.

"What, Lizzie?"

"You should cut our sandwiches like this for school. It would be fancy," she said.

Mam tried to hide her smile. "Yes, Lizzie, I suppose that would be fancy," she replied.

Mam gave them a small bag of pretzels and another package that contained two peanut butter cookies. They ate every bite, brushing the crumbs from their laps, folding their bag neatly and cleaning up after themselves. Mam smiled at them approvingly and put the trash in a paper bag.

Emma and Lizzie leaned back against the seats and tried hard to stay awake, but they soon fell asleep. Lizzie's head fell against Emma's shoulder, and as the train sped along through northwestern Pennsylvania, Lizzie was quite oblivious to the scenery outside.

Mam watched the girls sleeping and thought, *Even little girls who aren't going to sleep can fall under the spell of a moving train.* Especially if they got up very early in the morning.

Doddy Millers in Ohio

The evening sun cast a reddish glow across the train station in Baxter, Ohio, as the train came slowly to a complete stop.

Passengers stirred, slipping on their shoes and gathering their luggage as they came to their destination. Mam had all her suitcases and bags ready to go and was instructing Emma on which bags she should carry.

Before Mam could stand up to get the big suitcase, the white-haired gentleman was there to help. "If you will allow me, I will help you off the train, carrying your large suitcase," he informed Mam.

Mam looked a bit flustered, but she smilingly accepted his help. "As you can see, I do have my hands full," she said. "I really appreciate your help."

So with the white-haired helper leading the way, they made their way off the train. Mam followed, holding

Jason and a large bag. Emma held tightly to Mandy's hand, and Lizzie came last, carrying the small suitcase.

The black man smiled at them as they stepped down, touching his cap to Mam and wishing her a good day. Then they were on the concrete, a vast area filled with hundreds of people all milling about in different directions. It was a bit scary, but with the man helping them, they found their way to the door of the station.

Suddenly Mam stopped. "There he is!" she cried joyfully. Everyone stopped to see Doddy Miller make his way through the crowd. His white hair and beard with his piercing blue eyes were not easily missed.

Emma and Lizzie ran over to him and were enveloped in his welcoming hug. He held Mam's hand warmly, asking her if she had a good trip. Mam introduced the man who helped her with the large suitcase, and Doddy Miller shook his hand.

"Thank you for helping my daughter," he said kindly.

"It was a pleasure, sir. You have beautiful grandchildren. A wonderful family," the man said, and after shaking hands again, he left to find his own friends.

Lizzie looked down at her navy blue sneakers and felt beautiful. *That man was really nice,* she thought. Suddenly she felt something hard and smooth around her neck. She was being pulled back gently, and she knew instantly what it was.

"Goobity, goobity," she heard Doddy Miller say. Lizzie grinned up at him. *Doddy always does that,* she thought. He took his cane and pulled them in, saying that silly word that made no sense. It didn't even mean anything—except to Emma and Lizzie, it meant that their Doddy Miller was very special to them.

Doddy patted Emma's shoulder, grabbed the large suitcase, and together they all walked out to the parking lot. He had hired a driver, so they all climbed into an old, rusty blue car. It was so small that they barely fit in. Emma and Lizzie were not very comfortable, so when Lizzie pinched Emma to make her get over, they had a serious giggling fit. They were not allowed to make fun of this funny old car, but the harder they tried not to, the more they had to laugh.

Lizzie was very glad when that trip was over. They pulled in the drive to Doddys' house, and tumbled out of their confining space.

Lizzie just stood and looked. She loved Doddy Millers' home. The house was small, with a wide front porch. There were concrete steps leading up to the white porch, which was always cool and breezy in the summer. Doddy had a small barn where he kept his horse and surrey.

In Ohio, the buggies weren't made like Pennsylvania buggies. They were very narrow on the bottom, but bigger on the top, so that when you sat in a surrey, it seemed like you were going to fall out on the road, except that the side of the buggy kept you from doing that. Ohio horses were fatter and slower, and Doddy Miller was much more kind to his horse than Dat was.

Doddy also had a pet crow that talked. Emma and Lizzie were only a tiny bit afraid of it. Its round black eyes stared so hard that Lizzie couldn't look at it too long. It reminded Lizzie of something bad, like a picture of the devil she had seen once in a Bible story book. Emma said that crow was nice—it did not look one bit like the devil, but Lizzie didn't care what Emma said—it did—a little bit, anyhow.

If you opened a gate beside the barn, there was a little pasture for Doddy's fat horse. In this pasture there was a small concrete trough where a pipe came up out of the ground. Cold, clear water bubbled out of this pipe and into the trough. It ran through the trough and down a hole, running into the ground again.

Doddy told the girls it was called an artesian well. That meant if you tried to stop the flow of water, something would burst, because the water needed to flow all the time. Lizzie often wondered where it would burst if she stopped the water. Would it look like a picture of a whale, spouting water through a blowhole? Emma never let Lizzie try to hold her hand over the pipe, so she never found out.

Today Mommy Miller came out on the porch, wiping her hands on her white apron. She took Jason from Mam and fussed over him, admiring his curls and how much he had grown. Mam was smiling and nodding, talking as fast as she could as they carried the suitcases up the wide concrete steps.

"Oh, let's just sit here on the porch swing," she said. "It's so nice and cool here. It's just so nice to be here with you again."

"And to see you, too," Mommy smiled warmly at all of them, as she gathered Mandy in her lap. Mommy was small and soft-spoken—she never made much of a fuss. Mandy just loved Mommy and was almost constantly on her lap when they were together.

Doddy asked Emma and Lizzie to go with him to the kitchen. They hurried inside, and he handed them a bag of round pink candy. It was not hard and not chewy, just kind of crumbly. Emma and Lizzie were not allowed to look at each other or they would have burst out laughing. Doddy didn't know it, but they really hated that candy. It tasted exactly like Pepto-Bismol, that sticky pink stuff they had to take for a stomach virus.

Mommy's kitchen was painted white, with small white kitchen cupboards along one wall. The artesian well was piped into the kitchen, so the cold, flowing water ran through a metal trough. Mommy kept jars of milk, butter, and other items in this water to keep them cool. They had a funny, little white granite table with extensions you could pull out to widen it. The chairs were small and made of wrought iron in a curly design on the back. They were not very comfortable. There were bright-colored handwoven rugs on the floor.

Instead of a gas stove and refrigerator like they had at

home, Doddys had an old kerosene stove that Mommy had to light with a match. Their refrigerator was cooled with a block of ice that melted in a pan. Once a week a truck would bring them a block of new ice after the old one had melted.

Another thing Lizzie liked about Doddys' house was the bathroom door. It had glass in it that let in plenty of light, but it was so bumpy, you could not see through it. Lizzie thought it was a very smart thing to put in a bathroom door.

After the evening light faded, they moved indoors. Mommy lit the gas lamp, hurrying back and forth between the icebox and the granite table. She set out a big golden brown custard pie, and small, perfect oatmeal cookies.

Doddy made a big popper of popcorn on the kerosene stove, while Mam helped Mommy make hot chocolate. Lizzie was so hungry, she could hardly wait until it was ready.

After she got her cup of hot chocolate, she dipped three cookies in it, one after another. They were so good, she could have eaten another one, but she decided to eat custard pie instead. Her piece was large, and so shivery and golden yellow, she ate one delicious bite after another until it was all gone, even the soft, flaky crust. After that, she ate a bowl of salty, buttery popcorn and drank a glass of cold tea.

Then, as Mam and Doddy Millers sat and talked, Lizzie became sleepier and sleepier. She slid as far down on her uncomfortable chair as she could, but she just could not go to sleep on that chair, so she got up and walked sleepily into the living room and threw herself down on the couch. Emma soon followed and lay down on the other end. They had to arrange their legs so they both fit.

Sometime during the night, Lizzie felt a soft, clean-smelling blanket being placed across them, and she snuggled deeper into her pillow and slept on.

. . . . .

When Lizzie awoke, the sun was streaming through the living room window. A bird was singing in the pine tree outside, which sounded so pretty. Lizzie sat straight up, blinking her eyes in the morning sun. Emma stirred and mumbled in her sleep, pulling the blanket up over her head.

"Emma, get up! We're at Doddy Millers!" Lizzie said.

"Oh, yes, we are—aren't we?" Emma was wide awake, rolling off the couch in a tangle of pillows and blankets. Lizzie rolled off, too, landing on the pillows, and pulled on Emma's toes.

"Don't!" Emma said. "Stop that!"

But Lizzie was so happy to be in Ohio at Doddys, she just kept pulling Emma's toes, until they were both help-lessly laughing.

Mam appeared in the doorway, holding a bowl in the crook of her arm, stirring something with a spoon. "Good morning, sleepyheads! We were going to have breakfast without you. Guess what we're doing today?" she asked.

Emma asked, "What?"

"We're going to Uncle Homers for dinner."

"Oh, goody!" Lizzie clapped her hands. Uncle Homers lived up the hill from Doddys and had only two children, who were older than Emma and Lizzie. But she loved Aunt Vera, who always cooked great big delicious meals and talked all the while she was preparing it. Her house always smelled like frying chicken and stuffing. They had real bikes with only two wheels, not tricycles like Lizzie had at home. She could almost ride a real bike, if someone helped her a little.

Doddy came in from feeding his horse, and Mommy soon had their breakfast ready in the sunny little kitchen. The girls were allowed to eat without combing their hair or washing themselves, because they still wore the same wrinkly dresses they had worn the day before.

Mam said they were sloppy little girls, but Doddy just laughed and rumpled their hair, saying, "Goobity, goobity," in his teasing way. Lizzie looked up at Doddy's smiling face and loved him with all her heart. *He's the best Doddy anyone could ever have,* she thought.

They had a delicious breakfast of soft-boiled eggs and toast, with homemade pancakes and maple syrup. The maple syrup was much sweeter than ordinary pancake syrup Mam bought at home. Doddy said this was the finest syrup anywhere in the world. Although Lizzie didn't really agree, she never said so. It was awfully sweet—actually so sweet that Lizzie could never eat all her pancakes at Doddys.

Doddy even put it on his fried corn mush. Lizzie

could hardly watch him eat it, because it made her stomach flop.

After breakfast Mommy washed dishes while Mam combed the girls' hair. She pulled the snarls just as badly in Ohio as she did at home, putting Lizzie in a bad mood for a short time. They had to take a bath and put on clean clothes which Mam had laid out for them — green dresses with short sleeves. They didn't have to wear aprons because it was a warm summer day. Lizzie thought Emma looked really pretty in her bright green dress with her dark hair. Lizzie looked long and hard in the oak-framed mirror in Doddys' bedroom, but no matter how wide she opened her eyes, or which way she turned her head, her hair was not as dark as Emma's, and her eyes were different.

"Emma, do I look nice in my new green dress?" Lizzie asked.

Emma eyed her carefully. "I guess."

"What do you mean, you guess?" demanded Lizzie.

"Well, you're kind of fat, Lizzie," Emma said carefully.

"Oh well, that doesn't matter," Lizzie said, shrugging her shoulders. "Come, Emma—let's go see what Doddy's doing." And Lizzie was off.

Doddy was out in the pasture catching his slow horse. He led him into the barn and put the harness on, with Emma and Lizzie chattering to him as he worked.

The crow sat on its perch and watched them with its wide black eyes. Sometimes it tilted its head to one side to watch them better. Doddy was talking in a silly voice, and sometimes it sounded like the crow would answer in words of its own. Doddy's eyes would twinkle and he would chuckle whenever the crow did this, but Lizzie wasn't too comfortable with that crow sitting on its perch. She still thought the crow looked like that picture in the Bible story book, and it gave her the shivers.

They all packed into the surrey, Doddy climbing in last. He slapped the reins gently on the fat horse's big haunches, and he stepped out slowly. They turned left on the busy highway, with Doddy driving very carefully, as far off the road as he could, so cars could pass from behind. Emma and Lizzie got a fit of giggles, because they were squeezed together so tightly and everything went downhill to the right. They leaned so hard one way they could barely breathe, so it was a relief when they turned into Uncle Homers' driveway.

Uncle Homers lived in a low white house with a porch along the front. The grass was so thick and green it looked like a carpet. Brightly colored flowers grew in perfectly shaped flower beds, with birdhouses put neatly in little corners.

The door on the porch was flung open, and Aunt Vera came hurrying down the stone walkway.

"Oh my, I just told Homer, now you watch, they won't come in time to help me with dinner. And here you are. I'm so glad you're here. Annie, I do declare, you look thinner since you had Jason. Did you lose all your weight? And this is Jason. Oh my grounds. Isn't he a big boy already! Curly hair! Well, I would say his hair is curly—like a metal sponge!"

She lifted Jason down from the surrey. "You poor boy, what did they do to your hair? Annie, he doesn't look one bit like the girls!"

"Vera, he's our only boy—of course, he looks different," laughed Mam.

"Different? Why if I saw him sitting alone at the train station, I'd probably leave him there," she laughed back.

"Oh, here are my girls. Hello, Emma! Are you all better after having your rheumatic fever? I hope. Lizzie, how are you? Do you like Doddy's crow any better?" She laughed again, and hugged the girls tightly, including Mandy, then starting her endless questioning again.

Mommy was quietly smiling, pinching some dead flowers from a bright red geranium plant. She knew Aunt Vera would prattle on, so she took to the background and held Mandy, waiting until Vera's talking slowed down.

Doddy took the horse and surrey to the barn, and they all went into the house. The kitchen was large and everything in it was shiny. It glowed, with varnish on the kitchen cupboards, wax on the linoleum, and a glistening coat of white paint on the walls. Wonderful smells came from the oven, and a large layer cake stood on the countertop. The table was stretched out with added leaves, and a lovely blue tablecloth was spread on it. Vera had used her best dishes so everything would look pretty.

"Ach my, Vera!" Mam held her hands up in mock dismay. "You will never change. You shouldn't have gone to so much trouble, just for us!"

"Oh, I didn't, I didn't. I just told Homer, now they probably won't be hungry after Mommy's breakfast, so I won't make ham—just chicken and filling. And I didn't, no sir—I didn't make any ham!"

Mam threw back her head and laughed such a genuine, deep laugh that Lizzie laughed with her.

"Vera, I tell you, I'm sure you have plenty. You probably have five desserts, because you didn't make ham."

"No, no, I didn't! Just date pudding, but you know, it didn't get right this time—too dry. Oh, I made a nut cake and Jell-O. Some tapioca—nothing fattening, mind you. But we have to have pie. Can't have company without pie, Annie, you know! Just raspberry and apple, nothing rich. Nothing too rich this time," Vera stated.

So they all sat down to Aunt Vera's dinner. Uncle Homer bowed his head to say a silent prayer, and Lizzie had a chance to peep at his head. It was bald, except for a ring of hair around the large bald spot on top of his head. Lizzie knew it wasn't polite to stare, so she just looked at his head while it was bowed. She wondered why no hair grew there anymore.

When Uncle Homer looked up, everyone else did, too. He smiled his slow, quiet smile, telling everyone to dig in and help themselves. He teased Mam, and Lizzie could tell Mam was pleased when Uncle Homer teased her. Lizzie loved to hear them—it made her feel all warm and happy when Mam was so happy. Uncle Homers was just a place she liked to be, with all the good food and exciting things to do. Aunt Vera was, indeed, a very interesting person, because she hardly ever quit talking, and when she did, Lizzie wished she'd start again. She had an Ohio accent, which Mam said came from Switzerland, wherever that was.

chapter 20

The Keims

Today they were all going to Mam's other sister, Franie, and her family. They had to go with Doddy's slow, fat horse and his surrey again, and Emma and Lizzie looked at each other and smiled. That surrey was so tight full with all of them packed in together—they could not imagine driving very far like that.

But that was alright, because they were in Ohio with Doddy Millers and everything was fun—even crowded surrey rides. Lizzie had helped Doddy feed his horse and the black crow earlier. She decided the crow was funny, and didn't look too bad. She just couldn't look at its black eyes too long or she felt strange.

The water still bubbled into the trough in the pasture, and no matter how long they watched, it never stopped flowing. Lizzie wondered where all the water went, and if it flowed out of the earth anywhere again.

When they arrived at the Keim farm, Emma and
Lizzie were thrilled. Honks, squawks, whistles, and all
kinds of bird sounds greeted them. There was a pond
with weeping willow trees surrounding it, and rows of
pens that held lots of different bird species.

Uncle Dan was an avid bird enthusiast, so his farm
had lots of different geese, pheasants, swans, and other
interesting things to see.

The white farmhouse was set among old maple trees.
The lawn was kept neat, with flowers growing in bor-
ders along the house. The big white barn had a cow
stable and big Belgian horses that pulled the plow and
other farm implements.

The Keims had seven children, but only Hannah was
their age. Hannah was tall for her age and she giggled
easily when they were together. Ivan was younger than
Emma or Lizzie, and always tagged along, teasing them
and being a nuisance.

Uncle Homers arrived soon with their horse and
surrey. Leroy and Bertha were along today, too. They
were older than Emma and Lizzie, so they were a bit shy
whenever Bertha was there. She was pretty and almost a
teenager, so Lizzie was in awe of her. She was a bit shy
of Leroy, too, because he was a lot older.

The Ohio people dressed differently. They wore
round coverings that were stiffer than Mam's. Even the
little girls wore coverings, and sometimes they wore
black ones. Their hair was not rolled and combed back
sleek and wet like Lizzie's. They just combed their hair
loosely up over the top of their heads. Lizzie wished she

wouldn't have to have her hair pulled back so tightly, because the Ohio girls' hair was prettier.

Their dresses were made a lot different, too. Even their aprons were not the same. When Hannah wore an apron, you could hardly tell, because it was the exact same color as her dress.

Uncle Dan and Aunt Franie met their company at the door. Mam was so happy to see them, laughing with Aunt Franie about Jason's mop of curly hair. Hannah came shyly from behind Aunt Franie's skirts, politely saying, "Hello," to Emma and Lizzie. They smiled back, replying with a, "Hello," of their own.

"Do you want to go down to the pond?" Hannah asked.

"Oh, yes," Lizzie said eagerly.

"We'd better ask Mam," Emma said, in her responsible, grown-up way.

So they stood, waiting to ask Mam if they were allowed to go to the pond. All the grown-ups were talking so fast and so loudly that the girls could not make any sense out of anything. Hannah began to giggle, so Emma did, too, but it provoked Lizzie. She didn't know why the grown-ups had to talk so fast and loud. She yanked on Mam's apron, but she went right on talking. Lizzie yanked again and said, "Mam!"

Mam kept on talking to Aunt Franie.

"Mam!" Lizzie said, as loudly as she could without being downright rude.

"What, what? Lizzie, stop pulling on my apron like that. What do you want?" Mam asked with a frown.

Lizzie felt hurt and left out for some reason. How could Mam be so friendly if she talked so grouchy to her? She did want to go to the pond.

"May we go to the duck pond with Hannah?" she asked.

"Is someone going with you?" Mam asked.

"No."

"Then you can't go; not by yourselves," Mam said. Uncle Dan heard Mam and told her that there was a fence all the way around the pond because of the swans. He smiled at Lizzie. "Those big black swans could bite your fingers off if you provoke them. So don't try to go inside the fence, okay?"

"Alright," Hannah said, and they raced across the yard and down the grassy incline to the duck pond. There were all kinds of waterfowl living together on the pond. Stately black swans swam slowly by, leaving a perfectly-formed V of ripples on the surface. White swans swam in among the black ones, and different-colored geese kept to their side of the pond. There were big ducks, little ones, brightly colored ducks, and ordinary white ones. They all quacked or honked, seemingly taking turns. Lizzie watched them quietly, thinking the ducks and geese were more polite than Mam and her sisters.

Hannah and Emma sat quietly, with their hands clasped around their knees. The breeze blew Hannah's black covering strings across her face, and she flipped them back with one hand. Her hair was loose and little strands blew across her forehead.

Emma looked over at Hannah and asked why she had a bandage on her hand.

Hannah glanced at the bandage and her eyes opened wide. "Oh, Emma. I didn't think for one minute that you wouldn't know. Everyone else knows what happened to me, but of course, you and Lizzie wouldn't know." She took a deep breath and began.

"This isn't one bit funny. It was the most awful thing that ever happened to me." She coughed and started again. "You know my dad is a beekeeper?"

"What is a beekeeper?" Lizzie asked nervously. She bit her lip and looked around at the fence and the pond. Those black swans seemed enormous all of a sudden, so Lizzie quickly asked Hannah if swans could fly.

"No," Hannah said. "Dad clips their wings."

"Oh," said Lizzie, although she didn't know what that meant.

Emma told Hannah to continue her story, so Hannah settled herself more comfortably in the grass.

"Why, Dad has lots of bees living in hives."

"What's a hive?" Lizzie asked.

"Shhh!" Emma told Lizzie.

"A hive? That's a box, or a house where all the bees live. They make their honey in there. Every group of bees has one queen. She's bigger than all the others and the boss over all the bees in her hive. Well, you have to be really careful around all the hives, because the bees will sting if you get too close to their house.

"Every once in a while, the queen bee decides to move, I think, and they all swarm around her and fly somewhere else." Hannah paused for breath.

"Where do they go?" Lizzie asked.

"I don't know. Sometimes to a tree, sometimes further away—just different places, I guess. Anyway, I was walking to the hives to tell my dad supper was ready, and this big cloud of bees came flying through the air."

Lizzie's eyes opened wide. She pinched pleats in her black apron, and her heart beat faster, thinking about a whole cloud of angry bees. One bee was terrifying, especially if you stepped on one in the little white clover blossoms.

"Anyway, my dad started yelling as loud as he could for me to go back, and I did! I took one look at those bees and ran as fast as I could go, screaming as loudly as I could."

"Hannah!" Emma was terrified, just listening to her tell the story.

"Then, just as I reached the porch, a whole bunch of them settled on my head, neck, and back. They stung me many times—actually, about a hundred times."

"Did it hurt?" asked Lizzie.

"Of course." Hannah rolled her eyes, and slapped her hands on her knees. "It was just horrible."

"What happened then?" Emma asked, wide-eyed.

"Oh, Dad ran up and started scraping them off. They didn't all sit on me, just some of them. But I had to go to the doctor and everything. He gave me a shot, and I even had to stay in the hospital overnight."

"Did you really? Did you get another shot in the hospital?" Lizzie asked.

"Oh yes—two of them."

"Were you sore?" asked Emma.

"I hurt all over. It hurt for days, but I'm all better now. Except here on my hand I had an infection. So the doctor had to give me pills and stuff."

"My!" Lizzie sighed. "I'm glad Dat doesn't have bees. I'd be too afraid I'd get stung."

"Let's go over in the pasture and look at the hives," Emma said.

"No! You aren't allowed! I'm going to tell Mam, I mean it!" Lizzie yelled.

"Stop yelling!" Emma said.

"Well, you just said that to be big." Lizzie started to cry.

Hannah was so concerned, she patted Lizzie's shoulder. "Don't cry, Lizzie. We won't go over if you don't want to," she said kindly.

Lizzie was terribly ashamed of herself for crying, so she swiped fiercely at her wet eyes. She sniffed, bowing her head, and thought how unsafe the world was. That was just the trouble with living. You never knew what terrible thing might happen to you. Hannah was just walking along in the green grass, never thinking about a whole pile of angry bees. More tears welled in Lizzie's eyes, and she sniffed because her nose was starting to run. Everything just gave her the blues at that moment. Even the duck pond that had seemed so safe and serene seemed black and scary. The swans' eyes looked like Doddy Miller's crow's eyes, and Lizzie shivered.

"Let's go in," she said.

"No, I want to see where the beehives are," Emma said.

Suddenly Emma made Lizzie so angry she couldn't see straight. She got up, walked quickly around Hannah, and pinched Emma's arm as hard as she could.

"Ow!" Emma howled.

"You just want to go see those bees to make me afraid," Lizzie said.

"No, I don't! I just want to see a beehive!" Emma shot back.

"Well, then go! I hope a whole pile of bees sting you, too!" With that, Lizzie marched off to the house, wishing Emma understood how it felt to get the blues so bad you could hardly be happy about ordinary things, even if you were in Ohio. Emma just was that way—always happy and never being very troubled by anything. She just didn't understand.

Lizzie walked into the kitchen all by herself, standing against the kitchen cupboards with her hands tucked behind her back. She scuffed her sneaker against the brown linoleum and wished Hannah and Emma would get stung by one bee, at least. It was too bad to wish they would get stung by a hundred. That would be awful.

Actually, she liked Hannah, and besides, Hannah had been stung lots and lots of times, anyway. Just Emma could be stung a few times.

Aunt Vera stopped mashing potatoes in a cloud of steam. She bent over Lizzie and whispered, "What's wrong with my Mousie?" Her kind eyes twinkled down at Lizzie, and she looked directly into them.

"You're angry, aren't you?" Aunt Vera asked quietly.

Lizzie nodded her head.

"What happened?" Aunt Vera asked.

"Well, we were down at the duck pond and . . ."
Lizzie's lower lip trembled, so she bit down on it, hard.

"And then what?" Aunt Vera started mashing potatoes again, the steam enveloping her head as soon as she
took the lid off the huge stainless steel kettle.

"Oh, nothing," Lizzie said, and walked away from
Aunt Vera. How could she listen if her head was in a
cloud of steam? She wandered into the living room,
where the men were seated, talking and drinking steaming cups of coffee. Uncle Homer smiled at Lizzie and
she smiled back, going over to sit beside Leroy.

Leroy looked bored, reading an outdoor magazine. He
was tall and lanky, with eyes that were often half-shut,
because he was bored with the men's talk.

Lizzie wished he'd talk to her, so she sat over close to
him and coughed. He didn't notice, so she coughed louder. Leroy looked away from the magazine and watched
her with his sleepy gaze.

"Hi," he said.

"Hi," Lizzie answered.

"Are you Lizzie?" he asked.

"Mm-hmm."

"Are you the one Mom calls, 'Mousie'?"

"I guess."

"Why does she call you that?"

"I don't know."

"Where are Hannah and Emma?" Leroy leaned back in his chair and ran his fingers through his hair.

"Out by the beehives," answered Lizzie.

"Why aren't you with them?" he asked.

"Oh, I don't know."

"Are you scared of the bees?" Leroy asked, watching Lizzie closely.

"No, of course not," Lizzie said.

"You sure?" Leroy smiled.

"Yes."

"I bet you are. Do you want me to go with you, and we'll go find them?" he asked.

"If you'll go with me, I'll go," she answered.

"Alright." Leroy pulled himself up from the chair, and Lizzie had to look almost as high as the ceiling to see his face. He was even taller than Dat, Lizzie thought.

She felt almost as tall as Leroy when she walked out across the pasture to find Hannah and Emma. And

when he asked her if she saw all the swans down at the pond, she felt even taller. *Just wait till Hannah and Emma see me walking across the pasture with Leroy. They'll wish they would have been afraid of the bees, too.*

Hannah and Emma were not down by the beehives. Leroy said they would better not get too close, because the bees were active, buzzing around the hives. They stood side by side, watching the bees, until they heard someone calling from the house.

"Dinner! Leroy, come for dinner!" Aunt Vera called.

So Leroy and Lizzie walked back along the pasture, Lizzie pondering all the way how terrible it would be to have a hundred bees sit on your head.

When they reached the kitchen, Aunt Vera and Aunt Franie were seating everyone at the table. Hannah and Emma were on the bench, waiting for them. Lizzie slid in beside Emma.

"Where were you?" Emma asked.

"Oh, me and Leroy went to see the bees out in the pasture," Lizzie said.

"I thought you were scared," Emma sniffed.

"Not with Leroy." Lizzie smiled.

"Now you think you're big, I can tell," Emma said, poking her elbow in Lizzie's side.

"I talked for a long time with Leroy," Lizzie told Emma happily.

"So."

And when they "put patties down," Lizzie forgot to say "thank you" for her food. She was too busy thinking about how good it was for Emma that Leroy had talked to her.

Home Again

Lizzie loved going to Doddy Millers in Ohio, but it felt so good to be home again. Being with Dat, checking on Dolly and hearing her welcoming nicker, smelling the good harness smell from the shop, and hearing Mam's washing machine whirring all made Lizzie happy to be home.

Dat was making a new little pony spring wagon in the evening after the shop was closed. Lizzie was so excited about it, because Dat told her he might buy two miniature ponies to hitch up to this little spring wagon.

"How big are they?" Lizzie asked for the hundredth time.

"Oh," Dat answered patiently, "about this high." He showed Lizzie with his hand held very low above the ground.

"You mean they're so tiny?" Lizzie jumped up and

down and squealed. "Oh, Dat, that is going to be so cute!"

Dat just smiled and told Lizzie he had to finish the little spring wagon first.

"When? When are you going to buy them?" Lizzie wanted to know.

"I told you, Lizzie, we have to work on this first." He was drawing with a pencil on a piece of plywood and Lizzie could not imagine how he would ever finish it.

"How are you going to make the wheels? Won't that be hard to do?" Lizzie asked.

Dat pushed back his straw hat and scratched his head. "Now how do you think I would make wheels, Lizzie?"

"I don't know, Dat," she replied.

"I'll have to buy them from a buggy maker. They know how to make wheels out of wood, and I don't."

"How do they make them?" asked Lizzie.

"Oh, they soak wood in water until they can bend it, then they put a steel ring around it."

"How does the steel ring stay on?" Lizzie wondered.

"He puts bolts through the steel into the wood," Dat answered.

"Oh." Lizzie didn't really understand that, but she was glad Dat wasn't going to make the wheels. That would take him too long. She sat on an old wooden crate with her elbows on her knees and her chin in her hands. Her hair was not combed yet today and it was sticking out in every direction. She was wearing an old dress that was ripped at the hem, making it longer in the back. But Lizzie didn't mind, because Mam was busy doing laundry, folding clothes, and cleaning up the house since they had come home. Lizzie did not have to worry what she looked like. That was one good thing about coming home from Ohio.

Dat was measuring and sawing, whistling under his breath while he worked. Dat always did that, and Lizzie wished he would whistle louder.

"Dat, why don't you sing about Yugli?" Lizzie asked.

"You mean 'Yugli, vitt doo beer shidla'?"

"Yes! Do sing it, Dat. Do!" Lizzie sat up straight and squirmed on the wooden crate. "Sing it!"

So Dat stood up straight, laid down his pencil, and started to sing Lizzie's "Yugli" song.

Lizzie was delighted. She looked intently into Dat's

face while Dat sang the song in his familiar fashion. He sang it fast, and Lizzie's foot tapped in tune to the singing. Dat's eyes twinkled at Lizzie, and when he came to the part about the bull, they both burst out laughing.

Dat caught his breath, picked up the pencil, and started back to his work.

"Sing it again!" Lizzie said.

So Dat launched into another rendition of the old favorite and Lizzie thought Dat was the best father anyone could have. She loved him with all her heart.

Dolly's head hung over her door and she nickered to Lizzie. Lizzie turned on the crate and thought that was because she enjoyed Dat's song, too.

Mam and Emma walked across the lawn and into the little barn. "Melvin, your sister Sarah just stopped in and asked if it's alright if they come to sing tonight. What do you think?" she asked.

"Well, it's up to you, Annie. If it suits you alright, it's fine with me."

"Okay," Mam smiled. "Fine with me. I'll go tell her."

"Why didn't she come along out to the barn? I want to show her this little spring wagon I'm making," Dat said.

"She's holding Jason and reading a story to Mandy. You know how she loves the little ones," she said.

Dat stood up and smiled at Mam. "Yes, she'll soon have a houseful of her own, I'll bet." He grinned. "Is Aaron coming tonight?"

"Oh, of course," Mam said.

"Well, maybe I'd better clean up the barn if we're going to have company," Dat said.

So Lizzie helped sweep the floor, while Dat put away his tools. He stacked the pieces of plywood neatly against the wall, along with the wooden sawhorses he had been using. Every tool was cleaned with an old rag and put carefully on its hook or in the toolbox.

Lizzie loved to watch Dat clean things, because he did it so thoroughly. She thought she would be particular in everything she did when she grew up. Emma told her every day she was sloppy, but that was Emma. Little girls were allowed to be sloppy when they were still small, Lizzie thought.

After the barn was cleaned, Dat had some grass to mow beside the barn. So Lizzie wandered into the kitchen, where Emma was helping Mam make something that smelled delicious. It smelled a bit like popcorn, except a lot sweeter, and it made her mouth water.

"What are you making, Emma?" Lizzie asked, standing close to her and looking carefully into the bowl.

Emma snorted and stuck her elbow into Lizzie's stomach. "Go away, Lizzie—you stink!" she said.

"I don't," Lizzie defended herself.

"You smell like the barn. Mam, tell Lizzie to go wash her hands," Emma said.

"Lizzie, go." Mam turned from the stove and bent to smell Lizzie's hair. "You do smell bad. Where were you?" Mam asked.

"Just in the barn with Dat." Lizzie frowned.

"Emma, are you done stirring that? Here, let me see." Mam stirred the mixture in Emma's bowl. "Lizzie, you

go get the water started for your bath. And take down
your bob, too, because I'll have to wash your hair. We're
having company tonight and your hair smells like a
pony. Now go."

Lizzie did not want to take a bath. She knew she
didn't smell that bad; it was just Mam and Emma. She
knew if Emma wouldn't have said anything, Mam would
never have noticed how her hair smelled. Mam always
took Emma's side, that was all there was to it.

"I don't want to wash my hair. It doesn't smell bad,"
Lizzie pouted.

"Go on, Lizzie. Now hurry. Boy, making caramel
popcorn is a mess, or else this recipe isn't correct," Mam
said.

So that was what Mam was making. It did look like a
big mess—great hunks of gooey, golden-colored popcorn all stuck in big blobs. But it smelled delicious. "Can
I have some? I'm hungry!" Lizzie said.

"No," Mam said. "You're supposed to go get your
bath. Now go."

Lizzie sat on the kitchen chair and glared at Mam and
Emma. She did not feel like taking a bath and washing her hair one tiny bit. Mam and Emma were busy,
so they didn't notice the fact that Lizzie just sat in the
chair.

Finally, when they didn't see her, Lizzie walked
slowly to the bathroom. She turned on the hot water,
then remembered her clean clothes. She walked into her
room and yanked open the top drawer for clean under-
wear. She grabbed some, and pushed the drawer in as

hard as she could.

Dat wouldn't make her take a bath. Dat would not think her hair smelled like a pony. What was wrong with smelling like a pony, anyway? Ponies smelled good. And harnesses — Lizzie loved to smell horses and harnesses.

Mam and Emma were just like that. They thought the same way. *Oh, well,* Lizzie thought, *at least Dat thinks harnesses smell good.* She bet she should have been a boy. But that would be awful, having curly hair like Jason's. So Lizzie was very glad she was a girl after all, rather than look like Jason.

.   .   .   .   .

Later that evening, the house was filled with Dat's teenage sisters. They went to the youth's singings, and two of them had boyfriends — Aaron and Samuel.

They had gotten new songbooks, so they sang from those. Old songs and new songs and some Emma and Lizzie knew from school filled the kitchen. Then Dat got his harmonica and Sarah got hers. They played together, and sometimes they took turns. Aunt Sarah could really play. Lizzie could hardly hold her feet still; she played with so much rhythm.

Lizzie thought Aunt Sarah looked pretty. She had really wavy hair, and it shone in little ripples under the gas lamp. Her hands went up and down on the harmonica and her dress glistened in different shades of purple. Lizzie never told anyone, but once she had wet her hair and tried to make them wavy with bobby pins, so she would look like Aunt Sarah. It hadn't worked, so Lizzie decided your hair probably grew out of your head that way.

Finally all the singing and harmonica playing came to an end. Mam looked flushed and happy, serving the caramel popcorn, chocolate cupcakes with peanut butter frosting, pretzels, and potato chips. She also served steaming cups of coffee and tall, frosty glasses of grape juice and ginger ale.

Dat was enjoying the evening, Lizzie could tell. He loved being with his sisters, and tonight he was teasing them about getting married in the fall. "Sarah, how much celery did Mam plant in the garden this year?" he asked, his blue eyes twinkling at her.

"Oh, I don't know—not so much," Sarah answered, a pink blush spreading across her cheeks.

"Well, if you don't know about the celery, surely you counted the heads of cabbage. Or how many chickens are being raised in the chicken yard," he laughed.

"You just mind your own business," Sarah said, smiling. Aaron pretended to be upset with Dat, and hit his knee with his fist.

"You're pretty nosy, Melvin. Why do you ask about things that are just none of your concern?" he laughed.

Dat hit Aaron's knee and said, "Here. Now don't you start telling me whose concern it is. I'll surely have to help get ready for the wedding, and help the day of the wedding, and clean up after it. So don't tell me it's none of my concern."

They all laughed together, Emma and Lizzie joining in just because they were happy when Mam and Dat were

so happy. Besides, Mam had confided in them that Aunt
Sarah and Aaron might be getting married in the fall.
Lizzie hoped so, because they would be invited all day.
Marvin and Elsie would be there, of course, because
Sarah was their sister.

"Oh," Aunt Barbara said. "You haven't heard this
new song, Melvin. It's really a sad song, but we'll have
to teach it to you. You would like it."

So they all started to sing again. It was a long song,
Lizzie thought, because they sang verse after verse. It
was a sad song about a young girl who died and went to
Heaven.

Lizzie listened closely the first time, and felt very sad
and lonely for some reason. The second time they sang
it, Lizzie had a huge lump in her throat. She saw Aunt
Barbara watching her, so before anyone could see her
cry, she climbed off the bench and went into the dark
living room. There she lay on the couch with her back
turned and covered herself with an afghan. She held
her fingers to her ears, trying to stop the sound of that
unbearably sad song. Lizzie thought how awful it would
be to die when you were young. She would have to leave
Mam and Dat, and never see them again. Mam always
said Heaven was a much better place than here in the
world, but Lizzie did not think she would like it there
without Dat and Mam. She knew Jesus was there, and
Jesus was good and kind, but Lizzie didn't really know
who Jesus was, and she didn't want to live with Him if
she had Dat and Mam.

Mam said God was in Heaven, too, but Lizzie was

afraid of God. He was too big. He separated water, in
the Moses part of the Bible story book, and He could do
anything—even turn water into blood. And Lizzie didn't
understand how He could be very nice, because He sent
all those horrible grasshoppers and frogs to the people
who hardly did anything wrong.

So she lay on the couch and thought terrible thoughts
of sadness and loneliness, while great big tears squeezed
from her tightly shut eyelids. She cried until big sobs
and hiccups tore from her throat, feeling embarrassed
that she had to cry in the first place. Her misery increased when she realized they were all singing, quite
unaware of what had happened to her.

And then Lizzie felt a soft touch on her shoulder, and
Mam's face bent low over her. "Lizzie, sweetie, whatever is wrong with you?" she asked, as she lifted the
afghan from Lizzie's little form. "Come, tell me what's
wrong. You're sweating."

Mam put the afghan away, sat on the couch, and
pulled Lizzie onto her lap. Lizzie kept her head bent so
Mam couldn't see her face, but Mam's soft handkerchief
wiped her eyes and nose. Then she just sat and held
Lizzie against her chest. Lizzie slowly relaxed and her
sobs turned to soft shudders.

"Lizzie."

"Hmm?"

"Lizzie, they're done singing that song now."

"Oh." Lizzie wondered how Mam knew what was
wrong. Mam must be very kind to be able to know that
Lizzie had the blues about that song.

"Lizzie, it's only a song. It probably isn't true," Mam
said.

"I know," Lizzie whispered.

"And Lizzie, not very many girls die when they're
young."

"Don't they?" Lizzie sat up and leaned back to look at
Mam's face, in the dim light from the kitchen.

"No, Lizzie. You're not going to die. Every night
before Dat and I go to sleep we pray for you and Emma
and Mandy and Jason. Okay?"

Lizzie lay back against Mam's softness and sighed.
That seemed so very safe. If both Dat and Mam prayed,
that was a lot, and she was pretty sure God heard them.
So He probably took it quite seriously. Mam had shown
them a picture of a big angel helping two small children
across a bridge, with really scary-looking water tumbling over rocks way down below. So Lizzie guessed
Mam prayed like that, so angels would watch out for
them. But angels were scary, too. Once, in a story, a
man was so afraid of an angel, he fell on his face, so
Lizzie knew they weren't safe, either—not always.

"Do you want to go to bed now, Lizzie?" Mam asked.
Lizzie nodded her head. She was very sleepy because
it was getting late, and when Mam tucked her in the
cool, clean bed, it only took Lizzie a few minutes to fall
asleep. She didn't hear Mam and Emma when they came
into her bedroom a while later.

Mam helped Emma to bed and then stood quietly,
watching Lizzie sleeping innocently, her shoulders rising

and falling softly with her breathing. Mam breathed an extra prayer for Lizzie, knowing deep in her heart that a small girl who thought so deeply would need all the prayers she could say in a lifetime, however long God chose that to be.

School Days

Summer was coming to a warm golden end. The days were still balmy, but sometimes Lizzie heard Mam close the window in their bedroom at night.

School would be starting again in a few days. Mam was busy at her sewing machine every day, making new school dresses and aprons. She lengthened two of their Sunday dresses so they could wear them for school.

They went to town one afternoon with Evelyn, the Mennonite neighbor lady, and bought new sneakers, a pencil case, a tablet, and some new pencils. Lizzie begged Mam for a package of bright colored pencils, and Emma asked for erasers in a pack of eight. Mam let them have both, but she did not let them have a new coloring book, because they had plenty of them at home.

On the way home, they stopped at the Twin Kiss, where Mam bought them each a soft ice-cream cone that

was twirled. Half of it was chocolate and the other half
was vanilla. It was so cold and creamy, and Lizzie got a
bad headache because she ate hers too fast. Emma's ice
cream lasted a lot longer than Lizzie's because she ate it
more slowly.

Mam and Evelyn sat on the benches of the picnic
table and talked while they drank their root beer floats.
Evelyn had bright red hair and was tall and thin. Emma
told Lizzie she wished her hair was as red as Evelyn's.

"Why, Emma?" asked Lizzie.

"Because it looks pretty," she said.

"Yes, but just because it's combed up fancy and wavy.
If she had to wet her hair down and roll it tight, it would
look ugly," Lizzie said, catching the last of her melting
ice cream with her tongue. "Besides, would you want
her freckles, too?"

"I guess not really," Emma said, looking over at Evelyn's freckled arms.

"You do have pretty hair, Emma. Yours is almost
black and it's so shiny. I would be glad to have hair like
yours," Lizzie said.

"Do you think so?" Emma asked, dubiously.

"Of course, Emma," Lizzie said.

"Well, I like your brown hair better," offered Emma.

Lizzie looked over at Emma and smiled a genuine
smile of sisterly affection. "I'm glad," she said simply.

And then because the day was so sunny, Mam and
Evelyn were laughing, and all their new school things
were in the trunk of Evelyn's car, Lizzie put her arm
around Emma's shoulder and squeezed. She loved

Emma when they sat together and ate ice cream, especially when Emma said she liked brown hair better.

"I really wonder what our new teacher will be like," Lizzie worriedly told Emma.

"I don't know," Emma said, matter-of-factly. "Guess we'll find out on the first day of school."

. . . . .

That was exactly how it all turned out. Lizzie, Emma, and Lavina Lapp all walked to school together, as usual, the very first day. It was warm, but the leaves looked a bit dull on the trees, as if they knew fall was just around the corner.

Lizzie's new sneakers rubbed the back of her heel painfully. She tried to push her toes up against the front, but her shoe just flopped more than ever. She bit down on her lip, determined to be brave and not tell Emma and Lavina to slow down. They walked on, and the blister became more painful. Finally Lizzie could take it no longer, so she said in a very small voice, "Emma."

Emma didn't hear her so she said it a bit louder. "Emma!"

"What?" Emma stopped.

"My shoe is rubbing a blister on my heel," she asked, biting down on her lip so she wouldn't cry.

Lavina Lapp bent down to look at Lizzie's heel. "Ouch. That must hurt. I can see the blister through your stocking. Now what are we going to do?" she asked.

They all stood up and turned when they heard a horse come trotting swiftly behind them. A black horse was

pulled to a stop as a young girl pulled back on the reins,
scattering gravel as she said, "Whoa. Whoa."

A pair of very blue eyes shone down at the girls. "Do
you want a ride? I think you must be some of my pupils.
I'm Katie King, your new teacher. I'm late, so hop up,"
she said.

It was a buggy with no top. Lavina scrambled up first,
followed by Emma, and Lizzie plopped on the small area
on the floor.

"Come on, Roy!"

Lizzie's head flew back as the horse took a flying leap
and sped down the road. The horse's tail tickled Lizzie's
face, and the wind whistled in her ears as they went flying down the road toward the school. Lizzie didn't look
at Emma, because she was afraid they'd start giggling.

"I got lost this morning!" Katie King said, above the
wind. "I turned wrong at Clover Road, so that's why I'm
late. I should have driven more often by myself when I
was getting my school ready."

"That's alright," Lavina said. "We were early."

"I sure hope the other children aren't there yet," she
said. The new teacher pulled back on the reins to slow
down. They rounded the corner and came sliding up to
the schoolyard gate. Katie jumped off the buggy without
using the step, flung open the gate, and led her horse
inside. The girls all piled out, and Katie quickly unhar-
nessed, watered her horse, and tied him in the horse
shed. The girls just stood self-consciously on the porch,
because this teacher was very different from Teacher
Sylvia, who always came with a driver, and was much

slower and quieter than this new young girl.

Katie took the porch steps two at a time, inserted the key into the lock, and turned. She threw open the door and stepped back to let the girls enter first.

Lavina gasped when she stepped through the door. "Wow!" was all she managed to say. The schoolroom looked so different. There was a whole row of pretty scrolls with brightly colored roses, a different color for every grade, and all the pupils' names stenciled neatly in black letters. There was a colorful chart with all the primary colors on it and a chart with each child's cleaning chores and when it was their turn.

The floor was newly oiled, the desks were glowing with a coat of fresh varnish, and there was a new plastic water jug.

Lizzie drew in a deep breath, her eyes opening wide in surprise. This was like a different classroom. Everything was so new and pretty, and Emma and Lizzie walked around, touching things in awe.

Lavina was talking to Katie King, and Lizzie wished she knew what to say to her, too. But she didn't know what to say, so she just watched Katie from a distance, her hands clasped behind her back.

Katie was slender, with dark brown hair and a neat white covering pinned over it. Her eyes sparkled and danced with enthusiasm as she waved her arms to demonstrate a point. Her dress was gray, as was her cape, and her black apron was pinned neatly around her waist. Lizzie even noticed her shoes, which had small heels on them. Lizzie couldn't wait to tell Emma that Amish people could so wear heels, as long as they were not too high.

The door opened and the Zook children entered quietly. Everyone felt the same, Lizzie supposed, because the teacher was so new and different. One by one, the families arrived, saying, "Good morning," shyly, some with averted eyes. But Katie walked among her pupils, introducing herself, always smiling, putting a hand on one little girl's shoulder while she bent to talk to her at eye level.

Betty came hurrying up to Lizzie. "Hi!" she said, quite fervently, grabbing Lizzie's hand and squeezing tightly.

"Hi!" Lizzie answered.

"It's so good to see you, Lizzie! All summer I could hardly wait to come back to school, mostly just to be with you. Do you have a new dress on?"

"Mm-hmm," Lizzie nodded her head proudly.

"It's pretty," Betty said.

"Mam just made it last week, so it wasn't even washed yet," Lizzie beamed.

"Did you find your seat yet?" Betty asked.

"No."

"Let's go look which one has our name," Betty said.

Before they found their desks, the bell rang. Everyone looked for their name tag, and eventually the classroom became quiet as the children found their own desks.

As the new teacher stood at attention, she tapped a little bell on her desk, just as Teacher Sylvia always had. That was the only thing that was as usual, because her heartfelt "Good morning, boys and girls," was so loud that Lizzie jumped. The whole school responded much louder than when Teacher Sylvia had said it.

When she started to read her Bible story, she spoke very loudly and clearly, using lots of expression. No matter how hard Lizzie tried, she could not keep a straight face. She looked sideways at Betty, and Susie opened her eyes wide, lifting her eyebrows. But Lizzie looked away quickly, because she desperately wanted to be a perfect student for this new teacher. She clasped her hands carefully on her desk and listened closely.

The singing did not go very well because the pupils felt shy with a new teacher. But Katie smiled at all of them after she had put the songbooks away, and told them they sang nicely for the first time.

Then she introduced herself, saying this was her third term of teaching. She had taught two years at Rocky Creek School, about ten miles away. She asked all the pupils to introduce themselves and say who their parents were. After the pupils had made their introductions, the new teacher got Teacher Sylvia's wooden pointer and walked over to the wall where a new poster had been put up.

"Now, as you know, we need to pay attention all together while we go over the rules. We can't have a school running smoothly without rules."

Oh boy, thought Lizzie. *Here we go. She's going to have so many rules that I'll never be able to be good enough. She'll spank us little ones, I'll bet.* She glanced over at Susie, noticing that she sat up straighter, and her face took on a worried expression.

"The very first one, and by far the most important for all of us, is this one." Katie pointed to the first line. "Do unto others as you would have them do unto you," she said clearly.

"Now, if all of us would care more about our friend than about ourself, we would have a perfect school, and we wouldn't need rules at all." She smiled her wide, enthusiastic smile. "But since none of us is perfect, we will need rules this year."

Lizzie let out her breath. *Oh goody, she's still being nice,*

she thought.

"Who can read the next rule for me?" Katie asked.

One of the upper grade girls raised her hand and read quietly, "Please do not turn around in your seat or whisper to anyone."

"Oh, my goodness!" Katie raised her hand to her mouth in mock distress. "Is that as loud as you can talk?"

The upper grader blushed and giggled self-consciously. "No," she said.

"Alright, here we go then. Louder, please!" said Katie.

So the rule was read much more loudly and clearly, which caused the poor girl to blush again.

Lizzie trembled in her shoes. *Oh my. I certainly hope she won't ask me to read anything. She is too bossy,* she thought.

After the rules were read by different pupils, who all had to read them the second time to speak more clearly, Lizzie decided she did not like Katie King for her teacher. *How embarrassed that poor girl looked,* Lizzie thought. *She makes me mad. I'm not going to speak that loudly and clearly if she asks me to do anything—I'm too little.* So Lizzie drew her mouth down in a tight line, and sat in her desk, not liking Katie King.

The new teacher was quite unaware of one little girl's rebellious thoughts, as she moved up and down the aisles, distributing brand new tablets with cardboard backs on them.

"Write your name on the back, please," she said.

So Lizzie dutifully wrote her name on her tablet with her new pen.

That wasn't necessary to say, Lizzie decided. *We knew that last year. After all, this is my second year in school.* Without thinking, Lizzie leaned over to Susie and whispered, "We knew that, right?"

Susie looked frightened and held up one finger against her mouth, drawing down her eyebrows. "Shh!"

"Lizzie! It is Lizzie, right?" Katie stood directly in front of her desk, frowning down at her. Lizzie's heart flopped in her chest and her mouth went dry. She hadn't meant to whisper — she just forgot.

"Were you whispering to your friend?" the teacher asked.

"Y-yes. Kind of," Lizzie stammered, feeling perfectly horrible. *Now she'll just get out her ruler and smack me,* she thought miserably. She bowed her head and clutched the wooden seat of her desk with both hands till her knuckles turned white.

"Either you were whispering or you weren't, Lizzie," Katie said sternly.

Lizzie just sat there, not knowing what to say. It felt like twenty pairs of eyes were looking right through her, including the new teacher's.

"What did you say?" Katie asked, not unkindly.

"I . . . I don't know. I forget."

"Well, you must not whisper to your neighbor, and I hope everyone remembers from now on. Lizzie, I will have to let you go this time, but next time you will get a point on the blackboard. Now remember, pupils — *no whispering!*"

Since Katie stood directly in front of Lizzie's desk, her voice rolled out over Lizzie like thunder. Two huge teardrops formed in Lizzie's eyes and one broke loose, splashing on her black apron. She bit down hard on her lower lip, keeping her head bowed and wishing the floor would just open up and swallow her. She managed not to cry openly, but it was only because she thought very hard about the new pony spring wagon Dat was making.

At recess she got a chocolate cupcake from her lunch, unwrapped it, and found Emma at the water jug.

"Emma," Lizzie said.

"What?"

"Do you like our new teacher?" she whispered.

"I don't know yet. She seems a bit strict. But, Lizzie, why did you whisper?" Emma asked.

"I forgot we weren't allowed to," Lizzie said quietly.

"We weren't allowed to last year, either, Lizzie. You have to remember and listen to what she says."

"Okay." Lizzie hung her head. She decided the only good thing about the first day of school was her chocolate cupcake. It was big and moist and filled with creamy white frosting. There was a blue cupcake liner around it, and when you took a bite, you kept pulling the liner away from the moist, chocolaty cake. *Oh well,* Lizzie thought sadly, *I'll just have to be more careful.* But it did cheer her immensely when she thought of her bag filled with fresh cheese curls in her lunchbox.

Going for Groceries

It was Saturday morning, so Lizzie and Emma were allowed to sleep later than on school days.

When Lizzie woke up, Emma was not in bed beside her, so she knew it was really late. She stretched and yawned, snuggling down into her pillow again. She thought about the fact that it was Saturday, and wondered what they would be doing that day. She really hoped Dat would work on his spring wagon so she could watch. But she knew first of all they had to help Mam do the weekly cleaning. Of course, Emma loved to clean—or at least she acted that way. She was always bossier when they helped Mam clean, because she knew better how to do things right, Lizzie supposed.

She swung her feet over the side of her bed and sat up. She yawned again and scratched her stomach. Then, because she was just so lazy, she lay back down again,

and pulled the quilt over her shoulders. Maybe if she
shut her eyes every time someone tried to wake her,
Emma and Mam would do the cleaning all by themselves and let her sleep.

"Lizzie!" Mandy's tousled little head stuck in through
the doorway.

Lizzie didn't answer.

"Lizzie!"

"What do you want, Mandy?"

Lizzie couldn't help but smile at Mandy, even if she
didn't feel like getting out of bed. Mandy's huge green
eyes blinked at her like a little owl. Her hair stuck out in
every direction and she was still wearing her pajamas.

"Mam said to tell you breakfast is ready," Mandy said.

"Come here, Mandy. I want to show you something."
Lizzie smiled.

"What?" asked Mandy.

Lizzie hopped out of bed and hurried to her dresser.
She pulled out a piece of art paper that had some draw-
ings on it. "Look, Mandy. I made this for you in school
yesterday."

Mandy looked at it closely. "What is it?" she asked
innocently.

"Well, look at it," Lizzie said.

"Is it a puppy or a kitty?" Mandy asked.

"Not a kitty, Mandy. It's a calf. A baby cow."

"Oh. It's a nice calf." Mandy smiled at Lizzie.

"Do you want it?" asked Lizzie.

"Mm-hmm."

Lizzie took Mandy's hand and they went to the kitchen together. Emma was already seated on the bench, and Mam was putting Jason in his high chair.

"Good morning!" Dat said, looking up from the paper he was reading.

"Morning," Lizzie mumbled.

"Morning, Lizzie," Mam said. She brought a dish of scrambled eggs and a small plate of buttered toast.

"Is that all we have?" Lizzie asked, rubbing her one eye with her fist and yawning again.

"Oatmeal yet," Emma said grumpily.

"I hate oatmeal," Lizzie said.

"Then eat eggs and toast, and be quiet," said Emma.

"Girls!" Mam said sternly.

"I'll say," Dat said. "Everybody is not having a good morning."

"Well," Mam said, yawning and blinking her eyes, "Jason sure must be teething. I must have been up with him five or six times. So I'm not too energetic, either."

Dat looked at Mam closely. "You do look tired. I know what! I was thinking this morning, since it's one of the last nice warm days we'll have for a while, why don't we drive Red to town for groceries? All of us could go together," he suggested.

"Yes, let's," Lizzie agreed.

"Let's do!" yelled Mandy, and everyone laughed at her. Emma just smiled in her grown-up way and asked Mam, "What about the Saturday cleaning?"

"We don't have to clean, that's all," Lizzie said.

"Lizzie, we do. You just don't want to," Emma sniffed.

"If we wait to go till I get my cleaning done, I'll go

along, Melvin. But I do have to clean—this house is a mess this morning."

"Alright, then," Dat agreed.

So they all hurried through breakfast and the girls washed dishes while Mam took the broom, dust mop, and furniture polish with a clean old rag and started cleaning bedrooms.

Lizzie had her usual mountain of suds. Her stomach was soaked with warm, soapy water, and the soapsuds reached almost to her chin. Emma was carrying the dishes from the table, so she didn't see how much dish detergent Lizzie had used. Lizzie was washing dishes as fast as she could, and after the table was cleared, Emma got a tea towel to dry them.

"Lizzie!" Emma spied the amount of suds Lizzie had made.

"What?" Lizzie asked loudly.

"You know Mam has told you over and over not to use so much soap. Why don't you quit it? That's not even funny."

Emma drew out the word "even" until it sounded like "eeeeeven" and it just irked Lizzie so much. Especially since it was Saturday morning and all the cleaning was still to be done. But she didn't say anything; she just went on washing dishes in her huge pile of soapsuds. She knew that she was not supposed to lose her temper or she would not be allowed to go for groceries. Going to town with Red was so much fun, and she desperately wanted to go. So she just looked at Emma and said she guessed she must have squeezed the detergent bottle too hard.

Emma didn't laugh; she just snorted and held her nose higher than usual to dry the dishes. Lizzie felt so much like slapping Emma that it was scary. But she couldn't today, because they were going to town for groceries.

Mam came to the sink for some cleaning materials and sighed. "Lizzie," she said.

"What?"

"Why do you always have to use all that soap? You're just wasting detergent."

"I know, Mam. I told her not to, but she won't listen," Emma said.

"Dat says he can taste detergent in his drinking glass, Lizzie. Please don't use so much, and be sure and rinse them well today, since you already have so much in there." Mam hurried away, and Lizzie went on washing dishes.

"See?" Emma said.

. . . . .

The air even felt sunny, Lizzie thought, as they sat in the back seat of the buggy with the flap rolled up and secured with leather straps. They could look out the back window, because it was warm enough to drive with the windows open.

Sometimes a car would drive up close to the buggy and stay there, driving slowly because it was not safe to pass because of a hill or a turn. Then Lizzie felt embarrassed because she was afraid the driver would get impatient, driving so slowly. Emma smiled and waved, and if the driver returned the wave, Lizzie would, too. If the driver looked grouchy, Lizzie would yell to Dat, "Car!"

so Dat would get over off the road so the car could pass better. Lizzie always thought Dat drove too far toward the middle of the road. When they were in Ohio, Doddy Miller drove way over to the side and stayed there. But maybe that was because the roads were wider, too.

They passed a farm with two Amish women working in the garden, out beside the road. A chain-link fence ran along the top of a concrete wall, making a neat border around the garden. There were rows of pretty flowers, but the cornstalks were turning brown, and some rows of plants looked as if it was time to remove them.

The two women straightened themselves and waved. Dat and Mam both waved back as they went racing past. Dat had to hold back on the reins with all his strength, because Red wanted to run today. He did not want to be held back to a nice, steady trot. His head was held high, with his ears pitched forward or flicking back, sensitive to Dat's commands.

"I bet Red is going to fly past the stink factory today!" Lizzie said, gripping the window ledge with her fingers.

"Why do you say that?" Emma asked.

"Well, Dat has to hold on with all his power, I can tell," Lizzie said. "Didn't you see how fast we went past those ladies in the garden? It was almost as if we would have been in a car."

The "stink factory," as Lizzie and Emma called it, was a hide and leather company, or tannery, that was located on the outskirts of town. Red despised the smell of the rotting hides and would always pull on the bit and run as fast as Dat allowed, down the long, sloping hill, and through the underpass.

It was always exciting to Lizzie, because the closer they came to the factory, the faster Red would run. Today Mam said, "Now, Melvin, you'd better be careful. We have all the little ones along, you know."

Lizzie knew that Dat loved to go past the "stink factory" as much as she did. He always grinned a big grin, tightened his hold on the reins, and said, "Here we go!" just before he let them loose a tiny bit so Red would surge forward.

But today Mam and the little ones were along, so he kept a tight hold on Red. In spite of that, they sped down the hill and through the underpass, where Red's back seemed to flatten—he ran so fast. As soon as they drove out of it, the horrible smell came to their nostrils.

"Peww-wee!" Lizzie held her nose.

"Close the window, Melvin! Oh my, that smell is just horrible!" Mam complained.

"I can't now, Annie," Dat said, because he was too busy holding tightly to the reins. So Mam sat in silence so Dat could handle Red, and Emma and Lizzie held their noses and yelled because the smell was so bad.

After they were past the factory, Red slowed a bit, and Lizzie took a deep, clean breath.

Emma giggled, "Lizzie your nose is all red from pinching it so tight."

Lizzie looked over at Emma. "Yours is too, Emma."

"Are we there yet?" Lizzie swung around and stuck her head between Dat and Mam's shoulders.

"Almost," Mam said.

"What are we going to buy?" Lizzie asked.

"Groceries," Mam said.

"Just groceries?" Lizzie wanted to know.

"Yes, just groceries today."

"Doesn't Dat need anything at the hardware or the feed store or any other place?" she asked.

"No, Lizzie. Now go back. You're really bothering us," Mam said.

Lizzie flounced back beside Emma. "Boy, she's grouchy," she muttered quietly.

"She's not."

"She is."

"Well, you didn't have to stick your head way up there just to ask if we're getting groceries."

Lizzie guessed that was true. She knew Mam didn't like it if Red ran so fast past the stink factory, but she still hoped Mam was happy enough that she would buy them at least a Popsicle. Lizzie's favorite kind was a Creamsicle. It had creamy orange-flavored ice cream on the outside, and pure vanilla around the stick. Lizzie just loved them.

They turned down a side street, and stopped in front of a hitching rack that was located at the side of a huge brick building. There was one other horse and buggy tied there, and a row of cars were parked at the back of the graveled area.

"Alright-y, here we are!" Dat sang out. He jumped out of the buggy, reaching under the seat for the neck rope. He loosened the rein that held Red's head, and Red lowered it gratefully. He put the rope around the horse's neck and tied him securely.

Mam put on Jason's little cap, in case he got an earache. Lizzie secretly pitied Jason with his curly hair, and she wondered if Mam put his cap on because she was ashamed of it. She really hoped her own children would have straight hair.

Mandy hopped down into Dat's arms, and they all walked into the grocery store together. They got a cart and Mam put Jason in the little seat. Mandy sat in the bottom of the cart, and Mam pushed it down the first aisle. Dat followed with Emma and Lizzie, watching Mam put things into the cart. First, she stopped at the meat counter and bought a pound of lunch meat. She also bought some cheese and a package of hot dogs. Dat asked the lady for three huge dill pickles out of a glass jar. She smiled at all of them and asked if there was anything else today.

Mam said, "No, thank you."

"Have a good afternoon," the lady said.

"You, too," Mam said.

Lizzie told Emma the lady should actually have said, "Have a nice evening," because the afternoon was almost over. Emma said afternoons lasted till supper, and it wasn't nearly supper yet.

"Oh," said Lizzie.

Someone Amish came down the aisle. It was Dat's brother, Alvin.

"Hey!" Alvin said.

"What are you doing here?" Dat grinned at Alvin.

"Same thing you are. Getting groceries," Alvin said.

"Why don't you come visit us again?" Mam asked.

"Oh, I've been pretty busy at the silo factory," Alvin answered. "And," he whispered something to Dat.

"Mm-hmm. Yes, well, there are little ears around," Dat said, motioning with his hand toward Emma and Lizzie.

Alvin nodded his head and said something soft and low to Dat.

Lizzie became very angry all of a sudden. She did not like it when grown-ups did that. Little ears? Really. If they said things like that it always reminded Lizzie of little ears of corn. Which, actually, made her feel like a cornstalk with a little ear of corn on it. Dat shouldn't say such things, she decided firmly. She was going to have to tell him if they wanted to say things she was not allowed to hear, they should go away so she couldn't see them, not say, "There are little ears around." It just wasn't nice.

After Uncle Alvin promised Mam they'd come visit soon, they all moved on. Mam bought soap powder, dish detergent, cereal, and lots of other items, until Mandy was almost buried. She giggled every time Mam added another item.

Lizzie loved going to the grocery store. She loved to look at all the good food, wondering what some of the snacks would taste like. She was sure if Dat had piles of money, Mam would buy a lot more cheese curls and packages of chocolate cupcakes with chocolate icing on the top. They had white filling in the middle, Lizzie knew, because Dat had bought her one, a long time ago. Usually though, Mam made her own chocolate cupcakes, because it was cheaper. Lizzie supposed only fancy English ladies with high heels bought those packages of cupcakes.

"Excuse me!"

Lizzie turned quickly and hurried out of the way, pulling Emma back with her.

"Thank you!" An English lady hurried past, and Lizzie could smell the perfume she was wearing. It smelled so fancy. She wondered if Amish girls were allowed to wear perfume when they went to the singing. She certainly hoped so. This lady was not wearing high heels. Her shoes were white, and quite flat, so Lizzie guessed she probably had her high heels at home in her closet.

Jason started crying. Mam quickly gave him his pacifier, but he spit it out and cried louder. Emma picked up the pacifier and tried to give it back to him, but he only cried louder.

"Shhh!" Mam picked him up, bouncing him a bit, but he went on crying. "Oh dear," Mam said. Lizzie could tell Mam was becoming frustrated, because she told Dat to go ahead and push the cart, so she could take care of Jason. But Jason would not quiet down, so she took him out to the buggy and Dat paid for the groceries.

"Dat." Lizzie touched his arm.

"What?" he asked, putting a box of cereal on the moving belt.

"Can I have a Popsicle?" she asked.

"Not now, Lizzie. We already passed the ice cream

section and I'm already paying," he answered.

"Oh," was all Lizzie could say. She was so deeply disappointed she could hardly stand it. She blinked and felt a lump rise up in her throat. Emma was watching her, and Lizzie knew Emma wanted a Popsicle as much as she did. But there was nothing to do about it, because Jason was crying, so they skipped the ice cream section. That Jason, Lizzie decided right then and there, was a lot more bother than he was worth.

After Dat had loaded the groceries under the back seat of the buggy, they all piled in again. Lizzie and Emma were a bit quiet and subdued, because they had no Popsicles, but Mandy was chattering away to Mam, so nobody noticed. Or so they thought.

Dat untied Red and hopped into the buggy, and they were off. When he turned in at a gas station, pulling up along the side of the parking lot, Mam asked what he was doing.

"You'll see." He winked at Mam and asked her to watch the horse until he came back.

Lizzie and Emma hung their arms over the back of the buggy and stared gloomily at the macadam drive. They didn't even have a piece of chewing gum.

"Why didn't you say something before?" Emma asked. "You could have."

"Oh, be quiet." Lizzie felt like pinching Emma. It wasn't her fault—it was Jason's.

Suddenly Dat's face appeared in front of them. He handed them each a Popsicle, and gave them a little pack of chewing gum to share.

Lizzie was so happy. They unwrapped the Popsicles carefully and each took one tiny bite. The Popsicles were their favorite kind, exactly what Lizzie had hoped for.

"You spoil them, Melvin," Mam said with a smile. But Lizzie knew Mam was happy that Dat stopped for Popsicles, because she would have let them have a treat in the grocery store.

As Red trotted home, Emma and Lizzie ate every bite of their delicious Popsicles. Lizzie threw her paper out the window to the side of the road, and Emma scolded her terribly. She said you were never allowed to do that, ever; a policeman could get you for that.

After that, they divided the chewing gum, two pieces for Lizzie and two for Emma, breaking the last piece in half so it was perfectly fair.

"You should give me three," Lizzie said.

"Why?" asked Emma.

"Just because you scolded me," Lizzie said.

Emma said she just scolded her to teach her a lesson never to throw paper out of a buggy window.

Lizzie decided that was a good reason, and they chewed their gum peacefully the whole way home.

Teeny and Tiny

The weather turned colder, with a blustery wind ripping at the brightly colored leaves on the trees in the yard.

Lizzie thought that was the saddest thing she ever saw. All the golden leaves had to give up looking so pretty and tumbled to the ground, only to become all brown and ugly. After about half of the leaves were on the ground, Mam asked Lizzie and Emma to help her one evening after school.

She was putting on her sweater and scarf, putting her covering on the countertop. "The yard just looks a fright, girls," she said, shaking her head. "Would one of you help me rake leaves, while the other one watches Jason for me? It's just too cold to take him out."

"Watch Jason!" yelled Emma, as loudly as she could.

Lizzie looked up from her dish of chocolate cake and milk.

"Emma, I want to watch Jason. You can help Mam rake leaves. I'm too little," she scowled.

Emma blinked her eyes, lifting her nose just a bit. "I said first."

"Mam, right, I'm too little?" Lizzie asked hopefully.

"Well, I'm afraid not, Lizzie. You and Emma are very close to being the same size," she said. Then her eyes twinkled at Lizzie. "And, if you eat any more of that chocolate cake, you will be bigger."

Lizzie looked down at her bowl of cake and milk. The cake had fluffy chocolate icing on it and was swimming in cold, creamy milk. If you put just the right amount of cake and icing together with the cold milk, it was the best thing in the world. Especially when you came home from school and your lunch hadn't been very good.

Lizzie carefully cut off a piece of cake and soaked it in milk. She opened her mouth wide to fit it all in.

"Do I have to, Mam?" she asked, with her mouth full.

"Lizzie, don't talk with your mouth full. Yes, you can help me. Hurry up and finish your cake; I'm going out a while," Mam said, going out the front door.

Emma carried Jason into the living room to get his toys. Lizzie watched her go and wondered why she was allowed to be so bossy. She sighed, and ate another big bite of cake and milk. She supposed being a year older made a big difference, and besides, she didn't like to watch Jason that much anyway. All he did was cry or get into things he wasn't supposed to. If Lizzie put him in his playpen to keep him out of trouble, he really screamed. One time Lizzie pinched Jason when Mam wasn't looking, then ran into the bathroom when he screamed louder.

She tilted the bowl and slurped up her milk with cake crumbs in it. That wasn't quite as good, because there was no more icing to go with it. But she knew Emma would tell Mam if she didn't drink her milk. She found an old sweater and tied a green scarf around her head.

"Emma!" Lizzie said.

"What?"

"I hope Jason cries for you, if I have to rake leaves," she said, picking a white fuzzy off her black sweater.

"Lizzie, I mean it," was all Emma said.

But Lizzie felt better as she made her way down the stairs. If she had to give up, she could at least let Emma know how she felt.

Mam was raking long swaths of leaves, tumbling them all together in bright piles of yellow and orange. Her cheeks were flushed pink and her blue eyes were sparkling. With her dark hair and blue scarf, she made a pretty picture in the center of all the bright-colored leaves.

Lizzie found a smaller rake in the toolshed and half-heartedly swiped at a few leaves. They all stuck to the rake. She tried again, and a few leaves went where they were supposed to, but a lot more stuck onto the rake. She picked them off with her fingers, trying to throw them on the pile with the rest of the leaves. They blew back to where they had been in the first place.

"Mam!" Lizzie yelled.

"Lizzie, not so loud. The neighbors will hear you," Mam said.

"I can't rake these leaves. They just stick to my rake!" Lizzie frowned down at the rake.

Mam went on raking. "Don't worry about it—they'll just hang there to help push along the other leaves as you go."

So Lizzie went on raking. This just made no sense to her. Only half of the leaves were going where she wanted them to and her shoulders ached. She stopped and pulled at her itchy green scarf, because her ears felt like they were steaming.

Mam stopped to lean on her rake. "Whew!"

Lizzie leaned on hers. "Whew!" she mimicked.

Mam laughed at Lizzie. "You weren't even working very hard yet," she said.

"Oh yes, I was, Mam. You just didn't see me."

The shop door slammed shut, and Dat walked across the porch and down over the lawn. There was an older English gentleman with him. He wore denim overalls and a bright red cap. Dat was smiling and looking eagerly at Mam.

"Annie, this is Mr. Hudson. Thomas Hudson, right?" he looked at the man.

"Yes, that's right. Just call me Tom. Pleased to meet you," he said, shaking Mam's hand firmly.

"Tom, this is my wife, Annie, and daughter, Elizabeth," Dat said politely.

Mam said she was pleased to meet him, but Lizzie didn't know what to say, so she didn't say anything. She thought this must be a very important man if Dat said her name was Elizabeth.

"Annie, this is the man who wants to sell his miniature ponies. Remember, we talked about this before?" Dat asked Mam, a bit anxiously.

"Oh yes," Mam said. "I think we did discuss this. Or rather, we argued about this!"

Dat looked sheepishly at Thomas Hudson. Mr. Hudson threw back his head and laughed heartily when Mam said that.

"Well, I can see the Mrs. isn't too enthused about your idea of buying them," he said.

"I'm still trying to persuade her that it could be profitable, selling them later hitched to the little spring wagon I'm building," Dat said.

"Oh my, yes, it will be profitable. No doubt about that!" Mr. Hudson boomed.

The grown-ups went on talking, but Lizzie was rooted to the spot. Her fingers nervously worked knots into her green scarf, without even thinking. Her eyes followed Dat and Mr. Hudson carefully, listening to every word they said. She hoped so much Dat would buy these tiny little ponies, that she had to remember to breathe, because she kept holding her breath anxiously.

When Mandy came across the lawn, crying and asking for Mam, they all turned. Mam scooped her up in her arms, and tried to quiet her, saying, "Whatever you decide, Melvin." Then she told Mr. Hudson it had been nice meeting him, but she had to go get Jason.

Dat and Mr. Hudson walked slowly toward the shop, and Lizzie followed a polite distance behind them. And when Dat got his checkbook, Lizzie almost choked with excitement. She had to find Emma this very second. They were going to have two very little ponies!

She fairly danced up the steps, throwing open the door with a bang. "Emma!"

No answer.

"Emma!" Lizzie shouted, at the top of her lungs.

"Lizzie, if you don't quiet down right this minute, I'm going to have to spank you!" Mam said, her eyebrows drawn down over her eyes. "Don't be so noisy. Can't you see that Jason is asleep?"

Emma came out of the bedroom, closing the door very carefully. "Lizzie, stop being so noisy. I just put Jason down for a nap," she said quietly and in her most grown-up manner.

But Lizzie's excitement at the prospect of having two tiny little ponies was far bigger than being scolded.

"Emma!" Lizzie gripped Emma's arms with both hands, leaning forward so her face was only inches away from Emma's.

"Did you hear? Did Mam tell you? We are going to get two teeeeny tiny ponies to hitch to the spring wagon Dat is making!"

"How do you know?" Emma asked. But Lizzie could tell Emma was as excited as she was, or almost.

"'Cause. There's an English man here now. Let's go down and listen to what they're saying."

"Oh no, you're not," Mam said. "You're going to stay right here and help clean up the house while I get supper started."

Lizzie looked at Mam. Yes, she was grouchy, Lizzie

decided. She remembered now that Mam did not want
Dat to buy the ponies, saying she didn't think they could
afford them. So now Mam had to give up, and Lizzie
kind of pitied her, but not too much. Mam didn't like
ponies as much as Dat did, so she just didn't understand
how exciting this was. But because Mam's face was
flushed, and she was peeling potatoes with sharp, quick
motions, Lizzie knew better than try and change her
mind. Mam meant business.

As they crawled around the living room on their
hands and knees, picking up toys, Emma said quietly,
"Lizzie, when are they coming?"

"I don't know. Maybe tomorrow. Yes, I think tomorrow," Lizzie answered.

"But you don't really know, do you?" Emma asked
skeptically.

"No, not really. Actually, I have no idea," Lizzie said.

That really struck Emma as being funny, so they
giggled quietly as they went about their work. But they
had to be careful, because Mam was not in a very good
mood.

. . . . . .

About a week later, a bright red truck with silver-col-
ored sides on it pulled into the Glick family's driveway.
Dat was helping Mam burn great piles of leaves, but he
put aside his rake and hurried to the barn.

"Here they come!" Emma said to Lizzie.

Lizzie was way down deep inside a huge pile of
leaves. She was having so much fun with Mandy she
didn't even know what Emma was yelling about.

She popped up out of the pile of leaves, brushing them out of her scarf. "What?" she asked.

"The truck! Lizzie, don't be so dumb! The ponies are here!" Emma pointed to the barn.

Lizzie turned to look and saw the red truck. She couldn't think what was in the truck, so she just stood there in the pile of leaves.

"The ponies, Lizzie!"

"Oh! Are the ponies here? Oh yes, the *ponies*!"

Lizzie raced across the lawn, followed by Emma and Mandy. Dat told them to stay back until the ponies were unloaded, so they stood by the fence and waited until the truck was turned in the right position to lower the gate.

Carefully the gate was lowered by Mr. Hudson and his helper. The girls strained to see inside the truck, but it was pretty dark in there. Dat and Mr. Hudson walked up to the gate, and the girls heard a clicking noise as they untied them. Dainty little hooves bounced up and down on the bed of the truck, making it sway a bit. Dat appeared first, leading a little brown pony by the halter.

It was so little, Lizzie thought at first it was a dog. She put her two hands up to her mouth and squealed, without even meaning to make a sound. Emma was jumping up and down, with Mandy jumping too, just because Emma did.

Dat walked slowly down the ramp, followed by a tiny little brown pony. Mr. Hudson followed with one that looked exactly like the first one.

They were nervous, Mr. Hudson explained. "See,

they normally are much more quiet, but they're all excited today about their ride in the truck," he told Dat.

"They'll be fine," Dat said. He was stroking his pony in soft, smooth strokes, and the pony was nuzzling at Dat's suspender. "Lizzie, come say hello to the ponies," he called. Lizzie shook her head no. She wasn't really afraid of them, but she felt shy of the two English men. Besides, she was afraid those ponies would kick, because they were so nervous from their ride in the truck.

"Come, Emma," Dat said. "Come over and pet them. They won't hurt you."

So because Emma went first, Lizzie followed, being careful not to look at the men. Dat picked up Mandy and set her on his pony's back, but the pony moved away skittishly.

Lizzie watched the ponies, but refused to touch them, even if Mr. Hudson insisted they would not bite her or kick at them. Suppose they did? Then what? She would be terribly embarrassed with those English men watching her. So she stood staunchly, her green scarf tied securely under her chin, her sweater hanging loosely from her shoulders, and her hands clenched behind her back.

Emma reached out and softly touched one pony's nose. The pony reached out, following Emma's hand. Mandy giggled. Emma was enchanted at the touch of that velvety nose. She slid a hand under the silky golden mane, while the pony nuzzled the buttons on her sweater.

But Lizzie refused to budge. She waited until Mr. Hudson and his helper had put up the ramp, secured it

firmly, shook hands with Dat, and the truck had moved
slowly out the gravel drive.

"Lizzie, you act so dumb," Emma said.

"Well, suppose one of the ponies would have bitten
me? I would have had to cry, and those English men
would have seen me," Lizzie said haughtily.

"Lizzie, come feel how soft they are," Emma said. So
Lizzie reached out and held one pony's halter. It was a
bright blue halter, much softer and finer than Dat's halters in the harness shop. The ponies were so clean their
coats glistened in the evening sun. Slowly, Lizzie ran
her fingers through the soft hairs of the pony's forelocks.
She bent down to look closely at its eyes, to see what
color they were. They were a very light brown, and the
pony had long, black lashes that swept across the eye.
Lizzie thought she had never seen anything so pretty in
her whole life as these two ponies.

Dat stood back, watching the girls become acquainted
with their new ponies. "I think we should name them
'Teeny' and 'Tiny,'" Dat said.

"'Teeny' and 'Tiny'?" Lizzie giggled.

"Those are good names," Emma agreed.

"Alright. Which one is Teeny and which one is Tiny?"
asked Dat.

Lizzie stepped back to see if there was a difference
in one of them. She looked carefully, but there was no
difference. Dat and Emma walked around them, while
Lizzie held the halters, looking for a white mark or a
flaw that would distinguish one from the other.

"Here," Mandy said quietly.

They all turned to look and found Mandy pointing to the tip of one ear.

"It's white," she said.

Dat laughed. "Why, sure it is, Mandy! It is a white mark. Okay, this one is Teeny, because we discovered a mark first. The other one is Tiny."

Emma led one pony into the barn, and Lizzie followed with the other. "It's so nice they can be together in one stall," Lizzie said.

"Oh yes, you can't separate ponies like this. They're used to being together all the time," he said. He gave them a tiny bit of grain, and one block of hay, checking to see if they had clean water.

Dolly hung her head over the gate and nickered. Then she raced around her stall, kicking at the sides, tossing her head like a wild pony. Lizzie ran over and laughed at her. "Dolly, you big, clumsy thing—stop it! She seems so big now. Emma, come

here and look at Dolly. She seems like she's huge."

Emma ran over and laughed, too. "She does!" She looks like a workhorse compared to those little ponies."

"Come here, Dolly," said Lizzie. She sort of pitied her, because now they had two new ponies that were much prettier than plain old Dolly. But Dolly would always be special, Lizzie decided. She was a good pony, one that she and Emma could hitch up all by themselves and never feel afraid or anything.

Mam came into the barn, carrying Jason. He cooed and reached out his arms to the ponies, and Dat smiled at Mam.

"See, he likes them already," he said.

"Aren't they adorable?" Mam said, as she leaned across the gate with Jason to have a good look at the ponies. "Melvin, I've never seen anything like it. They're simply so tiny you can hardly believe it."

Dat took Jason, putting his hand on Mam's shoulder. "You just wait till I hitch them to my little spring wagon," he told her.

Mam pulled Dat's hat down over his eyes. "What spring wagon? I don't see one," she said, laughing when Dat pushed his hat up on back of his head.

"Oh, you will, you will. It's going to be the cutest thing you ever saw, Annie," he said. Then he looked at Mam so lovingly, that Lizzie felt like jumping to the ceiling because Mam did not care that Dat had bought the ponies. She loved Mam with all her heart, and she loved Dat and the ponies so much she thought she might pop like a balloon.

She guessed if everyone always loved everyone else, and everybody was allowed to have all the ponies they wanted, it would almost be as nice as Heaven.

She hoped with all her heart that her whole life would be as good as this moment, with Dat, Mam, Emma, Mandy, and Jason, in the little old barn.